# DEVILS AND THE DEAD

## ACCIDENTAL WITCHES SERIES, BOOK 7

## DEBRA DUNBAR

debra/dunbar

DANGEROUSLY FUN FICTION

# CHAPTER 1

## HADES

"Sir, I present to you my full report on the recent incident regarding the six missing souls."

Steve extended the spiral-bound document with great flair, as if he were gifting me his firstborn. The guy had even gone to the trouble of laminating a cover for his report. I took it, noting that his Photoshop skills had greatly improved, although he really needed to stop using Comic Sans.

I wasn't worried about the six souls—partly because they'd only been missing for less than an hour and partly because I knew why they'd vanished, what sort of event caused them to vanish, and that there was nothing anyone could do about it. I wasn't in charge of souls, their punishment, or anything to do with the operations side of the business. I was in charge of the firmament, the physical structure of hell, the rivers, and the veil that separated us from everything else. If I had to give myself a title, it would probably be Facilities Director. No, that didn't sound quite right. Facilities Engineer. Grand Designer in charge of Facilities. The Architect of the Afterlife.

Something like that.

Hell was supposed to be a one-way ticket kinda thing, but throughout the ages, some souls *had* managed to escape. Usually that was due to crappy wording on a crossroad demon's contract, or a special bargain, or a little internal corruption.

Sometimes it was due to necromancy. But no one really wanted to admit that. It was easier for the demons to point fingers at each other and send some poor scapegoat off to a pot of boiling oil for a century than admit a human could snatch a soul out from under our noses and we could do pretty much nothing about it.

At times, the finger pointing turned my way. They'd claim there must be a crack in the firmament, a tear in the veil, a narrow spot in the river that allowed souls to leave hell. When that happened, I'd shrug and tell them to show me the weakness. No one wanted to spend eons going over every inch of hell for an escape route, so they'd immediately go back to blaming each other and leave me blissfully alone.

Then Steve had come along. Fifty years ago Satan had decided I needed an assistant. One of his human worshipers had died, and personnel hadn't been sure what to do with him. There weren't any openings in the fifth or eighth circles. None of the executives wanted to bring him on as a member of their staff. We couldn't toss him in with the rest of the sinners after a lifetime of exemplary work honoring the Dark Lord. So I got stuck with him.

Clearly I was being punished for something.

"If you'll note here, sir." Steve leaned over my desk to flip the report open. "The souls vanished from their stations at exactly the same time. They don't reside in the same circles. They don't have sins in common with each other. But, through some diligent research, I discovered that they are all related. The Hoffman family."

"I see." Satan save me from overzealous underlings.

"But!" He turned a few pages and jabbed a bony finger at the page. "Not all members of this Hoffman family left hell. Just this subset. *How very curious*, I thought to myself."

"Yes, I'm sure you did." I glanced up at the clock, wondering if I was going to make my ten-thirty tee time.

"I took the liberty of asking Purgatory if anything similar had happened to them. My source confirmed that two souls also vanished the exact same hour as ours, and that they too were related to the same Hoffman family."

"You *what?*" Steve was going to be the death of me. We shouldn't be exchanging confidential information with anyone outside of hell—especially purgatory and heaven. Yes, it was interesting that purgatory had the same problem, but that information wasn't worth revealing that six of hell's souls had momentarily poofed out of their circles.

Steve held up a hand. "My source is very discreet. They also told me it was rumored that several souls vanished from heaven at the exact same time—also from the Hoffman family."

I sat back in my chair, intrigued. Purgatory and heaven had the same missing-soul issue as hell. That would definitely help if the finger of blame was pointed my way again. The problem couldn't be with our structure and facilities. Although this sort of thing indicated a flaw at the top of the food chain. A design flaw. And since neither Satan nor his father were disposed to accepting blame for anything, it would probably end up in my lap at the end of the day. I picked up the report, wondering if I needed to cancel my golf outing or if I could still manage to squeeze in a quick nine after lunch.

Steve snatched the report out of my hands, turning it to the back page and pointing once more. "See? All of them were Hoffmans. Not all Hoffmans were taken. *But* every one of the souls who vanished was buried in *this* family cemetery on *this* farm. That's the big link." Steve plopped the report on my desk and stood back, his posture radiating smug satisfaction.

Steve was definitely crossing some insubordination lines here. Normally such behavior would have warranted disciplinary action, but for once I agreed with Steve. This was big. Really big.

A family cemetery. Over eight souls from all realms of the afterlife, all of whom were buried in one location. This wasn't random or an escape assisted by a demon on the take. No, this was the work of magic.

It was the work of a necromancer.

I'd suspected as much, and it was gratifying to have those suspicions bolstered a bit, but at the end of the day, this really had nothing to do with me. These souls who'd temporarily left their afterlife hadn't done so because of any design flaw in hell or purgatory. They hadn't left because of a weakening in the veil, or a crumbling of the infrastructure. They'd been summoned by a necromancer.

It wasn't my problem. Which meant I was absolutely going to make my tee time this morning.

## CHAPTER 2

### BABYLON

loved working nights. I loved watching the drunk humans stagger through the parking lot at closing time, embracing someone they'd probably be sneaking away from at dawn.

Standing at the door I watched the couple in the parking lot. "Have fun! Make good choices. Use a condom," I shouted to them.

It had been a long time since I'd done that. Gone home with a hot guy, that is. I'd thought I'd found the man of my dreams and had put aside all those one-night-stands to focus on our relationship. But the man of my dreams turned out to be a nightmare, and although it had been six months since he'd ghosted me, I just couldn't go back to the carefree, casual sex I'd once enjoyed.

With a sigh, I finished locking the door, still watching Patty and her man-of-the-evening as they climbed into their Lyft ride. I needed time for my bruised heart to heal. And I knew deep down that for me, healing wouldn't come by jumping into the sack with some random guy.

Patty and her own random guy drove off. I turned to survey the mess I needed to clean up before I went home.

"At least tips were good." Kristin swept a dozen empty bottles into a trash can and began to scrub down the table top.

We'd run our asses off tonight, understaffed and coping with an unexpected crowd. I didn't mind the hard work if I rolled in the kind of dough I'd made tonight. Kristin and I would set the place to rights, and I'd be home by three, blackout curtains firmly in place so I could sleep in past noon. The schedule showed me working tomorrow night, then off for Sunday and Monday, and I was already dreaming of spending them without pants, sprawled in front of the television, eating whatever my chosen delivery brought to my door. Maybe I'd freshen up my hair color a bit. Turning my natural auburn hair into glossy locks of fire-engine red meant regular maintenance. Touch up the do, binge old sitcoms, and not see the light of day, or night, for forty-eight hours. That was the plan, and I was sticking to it.

"Hey, there's a guy at the door," Kristin announced. "Should I let him in? He's kinda beefy, and we already let Ricky go home for the night."

Ricky was our bouncer. I made my way back to the door, because while Kristin might hesitate to let in a guy that outweighed her by eighty pounds, I wouldn't. Not that I was any use at all in a physical fight, but if beefy-dude tried anything, I'd sic the ten undead rats from the storeroom on him. I don't care how tough a man is, a swarm of decomposing rodents is gonna make him scream in soprano and run for the hills.

Undead stuff was my jam. I was the youngest of the Perkins witches, and I'd been gifted with the freakiest magic. Necromancers were rare. Technically it wasn't even a witch skill, but it was *my* skill and I'd never really bothered to question the why or the how of it. Ever since I'd been in the cradle, I'd been animating the dead. The bar where I worked had a bit of a pest problem, and the poison traps set out all over the storeroom meant there were lots of dead for me to animate. There was a guy who came in every few days supposedly to dispose of the bodies, but he never found any of them.

I made sure he never found any of them.

My little undead army. Normally I stuck to insects and animals, because animating humans took a real toll on me, but a few weeks ago I'd needed to raise a bunch of dead to defend my sister, my friends, and me against some nasty demons. There'd been too much going on to keep track of all the dead, so I'd crossed a line I didn't usually cross. I'd zomb-ified them.

Animated dead are like puppets that I control. Zombies I can give instruction to and turn loose. They manage completely on their own. It's easier for me, but it involves calling a portion of their soul back into the body. According to my sisters, it was a morally gray area, but according to them everything I did was a morally gray area. In the past, nothing horrible had ever happened when I'd created zombies, but I'd always tried to save that activity for emergencies only.

Unlocking the heavy door, I swung it open to see that Kristin was right. There was a beefy dude on the other side. He was about six foot three and a solid wall of muscle clad in jeans and a flannel shirt. Curls of chest fur poked out of the open neck of his shirt. His hair was slicked back either from gel or the cold rain that had started to come down. Dark stubble was the only thing darkening his chin and jaw, meaning he'd probably shaved at least three times today. His hands twisted a ball cap between them.

"Hi Babylon. Can I come in?"

"Clinton!" I stood aside and let the werewolf into the bar, catching his damp, earthy scent as he passed me. "We're closed for the night."

Not that the werewolf was probably here for a beer and the music. I lived outside the limits of Accident—the town where supernatural creatures felt free to openly live their lives, protected and guarded by the wards and magic of generations of Perkins witches. A few supes occasionally hung out in the human world, but not werewolves. They were like some incredibly paranoid cult, living mostly secluded lives in their packs and avoiding humans. There were some werewolves in Accident who'd never seen a human in their entire lives. There were some who'd not only never journeyed outside Accident, they'd never left their pack territory.

Clinton was the Alpha of a splinter pack that had broken off from his father's main one. The whole thing had nearly caused a war and a ton of bloodshed, but somehow all that had been avoided. The two packs now lived on different mountains, socializing and hunting on common lands during full moons and shifter holidays. So having Clinton show up in a human bar outside of Accident was a bit of a shock.

"Is this a friend of yours?" Kristin sashayed up to us holding a broom. She liked muscle-bound guys, and she knew I didn't. That made Clinton fair game in her book.

Clinton's eyes grew huge. The poor guy was terrified. Centuries of isolation after being once hunted down and targeted for extermination meant the werewolves weren't just suspicious of humans, they were afraid of them. The big alpha looked as if he were about to bolt right back out the front door. I put a hand on his arm, trying to calm him down a bit.

"This is my co-worker, Kristin. Kristin, this is Clinton. He's gay."

Clinton wasn't gay that I was aware of, but my labeling him as such had the desired effect. Kristin's mouth turned into a pout and she headed back to her cleaning, muttering something about how it just figured.

I waited a few seconds for the werewolf to turn his attention away from the potential threat and to me. "What's up?"

He went back to twisting his hat. "I'm hoping you can help my pack and me up on Savior Mountain."

"With construction?" With the assistance of everyone in Accident, Clinton's pack had managed to get buildings up and under roof, wells dug, solar power online, and some basic roadways done before the weather had turned. There was still a lot of work for them to do, but I wasn't the one to help them with that. Hammering nails and hanging drywall were at the bottom of my skills list.

"No." The hat tore in two, and Clinton looked down at the pieces as if he were baffled about how it had happened. "We've got a ghost problem."

"Ghosts?" Werewolves were very superstitious, but I've never heard any of them claim to have seen the spirits of the dead.

"At night we see them down by the road, over by the river, and even in our own homes. Sometimes they knock things over. Flick claims one spoke. It said something about Christmas decorations being missing."

I shook my head. "I can speak with the dead and sometimes convince them to return to rest, but I'm not a skilled medium, Clinton. Ghosts aren't really my thing."

"Dead is your thing, though." Clinton put the torn pieces of hat on a nearby table. "You're a necromancer. A witch and a necromancer. You make the dead rise up. Ghosts are dead."

"Yeah, but ghosts are spirits, not dead bodies." I held my hands up. "My magic animates the dead. That doesn't involve helping them find their lost Christmas decorations."

"But you return the dead to the grave when you're done with them. Can't you do the same to ghosts?"

I opened my mouth to say no, then snapped it shut. In all honesty, I could. It just wasn't something I did on the regular. I'd seen plenty of ghosts in my lifetime. It was what had given me the idea of trying to do more than just animate a corpse. Some spirits were clearly souls that had refused to move on, preferring to hang around here without a body, but those were rare. Most ghosts were just echoes of their former selves, performing a certain action over and over again, always at the same time and same place. Others could occasionally be communicated with and had the ability to somewhat vary their patterns.

When I was a kid, I'd realized that if a soul could journey to the afterlife, but leave a spirit-sized portion behind to knock over pictures and vases, then I could use that spirit to power its own dead body. Then I'd gone from using existing ghosts to summoning them. It had been ridiculously easy to pull a portion of a soul from the afterlife, create a ghost, then use the ghost to animate the body.

Of course, returning the ghost could prove to be a problem, as I'd discovered two weeks ago. That was what made me reluctant to promise Clinton help with his issue. If I failed to send my own self-summoned spirit across the veil, I might fail to do the same to ghosts I hadn't brought into being myself. Banishing...well, it was hit or miss with me. And given my recent track record, I was probably more likely to miss than to hit.

"I'm not promising anything, Clinton," I warned him. "I'll give it a shot, but I don't know if I can help you."

His face split with a relieved grin. "That's all I'm asking, Babylon."

"Am I gonna clean this place all by myself?" Kristin shouted over.

I pushed Clinton into a chair, where he sat as I started wiping down tables. To the werewolf's credit, he got right back up again, picked up a washrag of his own, and pitched in. It was weird how much Clinton had changed in the last year. He used to be that big redneck asshole who only came into town to get drunk, fight, and cause trouble, but ever since he'd become the alpha of his own pack, Clinton had developed manners along with a sense of responsibility.

"Why didn't you go to Cassie with your ghost problem?" I asked him as I filled the mop bucket.

My eldest sister was the most powerful witch of the seven of us, and although we all helped, she was really the witch who ran Accident, the one with the recognized authority to decide who was allowed to stay and who was told to leave.

Clinton shook his head. "I've gone to Cassie for a whole lot this year. I don't want to be seen as someone who runs to her with every problem. Makes me look weak."

"But running to me doesn't?" I shut off the water and hauled the bucket to the floor.

"Asking you for help is like calling in an outside consultant," he explained. "Cassie is another alpha. Alphas assisting each other isn't a problem, but if the assistance starts to look one-sided, my pack might start to see me as a step below Cassie, which means they'd also see me as a step below my father."

Werewolf hierarchies were important, and always changing. I didn't think Clinton had anything to worry about, but what did I know? I wasn't a shifter.

"Besides, I didn't exactly *run* to you. I drove." Clinton grinned. "And I knocked."

Definitely a kinder and gentler Clinton than the one I'd grown up with. "So tell me more about these ghosts. Do they only appear at night? What sort of things are they knocking off shelves and walls? And exactly what did the one Flick spoke to say about missing Christmas decorations?"

"This is so cool," Kristin interjected. "Hauntings and seances and shit. I had no idea you did this on the side, Lonnie."

I grimaced. My human friends didn't know I was a witch and certainly didn't know about my gruesome magical specialty. They just saw me as that kinda weird goth girl who had a bunch of sisters, collected bones, and made an awesome margarita. Hopefully Kristin wouldn't spread the word because I didn't want to be inundated with requests from randos to contact their long dead uncles and aunts.

"Flick said the ghost couldn't rest until it found the lost tinsel, or something like that. Flick was kinda shook up, so I can't guarantee that was the ghost's exact words, but it was the general gist of the conversation."

Tinsel. A sparkly Christmas tree decoration. Had the ghost been obsessed with the holiday? I didn't know all that much about poltergeists, but I got the idea that those trapped in the mortal plane might harp on whatever had been important to them in life, and not just recreate their deaths, or look for some sort of vengeance or resolution of what might have been an outstanding issue at the time they'd died.

But from what I'd gleaned, ghosts tended to haunt either the spot where they died, or a place they'd lived. No one had lived at spirit mountain aside from that group of elves. The elves had abandoned the mountain decades ago. There weren't a lot of places where fae felt comfortable setting up residence, so everyone had assumed they'd gotten tired of living in Accident and returned to their homeland. It couldn't be the elves haunting the mountain. They were immortal, or so long-lived they might as well have been immortal. But outside the elves, the only beings in the past that had called Savior Mountain home were animals—and a badger shifter.

Maybe it wasn't a former resident that was haunting the place, but someone who had died on the mountain. Had the elves killed someone and buried them close to where Clinton and his pack had set up shop? If so, it had to have been someone from outside of Accident. I glanced over at Clinton, remembering the uproar when *he'd* gone missing. Even the most isolated resident had people who would notice if they suddenly just didn't come home, or show up, one day.

Still, none of that explained the ghost's need to locate missing Christmas decorations.

"Five households have reported items being knocked over or disappearing. There doesn't seem to be any pattern to these. Things like pictures, books, candles, kitchen utensils. Rose had an apple pie vanish, but I'm not positive that was a ghost."

I'd had Rose's apple pie. If she'd put it out on the porch to cool, it's no wonder it wasn't there when she came back. Any of the werewolves might have stolen it, and I couldn't really see a ghost taking an apple pie. It's not like they could eat it, and transporting a physical object took a heck of a lot more ghostly skill than just knocking a candle off a shelf.

"The ghost sightings are always at night. If you come out, I can show you where they were. Even with our night vision, no one was able to recognize the ghost or even tell what it really was. Reports are that they're humanoid, and four to five feet tall, and that they move fast. Kinda flitting around is what Bertram said."

I thought as I mopped the floor. Four to five feet tall? So ghosts of children? I shuddered, not really wanting to consider that. Maybe they were really short people. Or maybe they weren't human at all. Lots of the supernaturals who called Accident their home were on the short side.

"I'll come out tomorrow around lunch time," I told Clinton. If the situation warranted it, I'd make arrangements to stay the night on Sunday, and maybe I could get up close and personal to one of these ghosts. So much for two days of pajamas and television.

"Thanks Babylon. I really appreciate it."

Clinton picked up the garbage bags and took them out to the dumpster out back. Kristin watched him go and sighed.

"You sure he's gay?"

"One hundred percent," I lied.

The werewolf stayed and helped us clean up, which was absolutely not something he would have done a year ago. The guy even waited for Kristin and me to lock the door, and made sure we were safely in our cars before leaving. I'd grown up thinking the werewolves were assholes. Now I thought differently. Yeah, some were still assholes. I really wasn't fond of Clinton's father, Dallas, although his new wife Tink was a hoot. But whether I liked them or not, I was a Perkins witch, and taking care of Accident was kind of my birthright. If I couldn't help Clinton myself, I'd research, ask my sisters for assistance, and find someone who could do the job. It's what we did. Few seldom called upon me and my weird magic, and in all honesty I was kind of flattered Clinton had turned to me.

# CHAPTER 3

## HADES

"We've got a problem." Eshu wrung his hands together, looking upward.

I eyed him over the blueprints for a project to improve the Cliffs of Despair and increase the misery, making them even more hopeless. The demon before me acting out the Cassandra routine wasn't actually a demon. He was older than Satan himself, and on par in power and abilities with the dark lord, although you'd never know it from the way he acted. Eshu was our messenger—which was a more important role than it sounded. He was the only being who could freely go between heaven, hell, and purgatory, as well as the mortal realm. Convenient, but as he was also a bit of a trickster, the messages, both sent and received, were often not quite what was intended.

"Go on. Tell me the problem," I prompted, knowing he wouldn't reveal this information unless asked.

"Remember the souls that were summoned away, only to be returned after a couple of hours?"

I nodded, musing over the blueprints as I listened.

"Well, one didn't come back."

I looked up once more. "Nonsense. I personally counted them. Six. They all came back."

Eshu smirked. "Hell's returned. Purgatory's returned. Not all of heaven's returned."

I shrugged, not really caring if heaven was missing a soul or not. "Sucks to be them."

"They're pissed. They're blaming hell."

That got my attention. "Hell had souls vanish as well. Why would they think hell had something to do with it?"

It was Eshu's turn to shrug. "Maybe because they're the one missing a soul and we're not? Either way, there's an emergency meeting right now, and the boss wants you there."

"Me?" This had to have been one of Eshu's mistakes. Satan had said to send his son, Lucien, and somehow in that rollercoaster of a brain, Eshu had heard Hades.

"You."

This was ridiculous. I had no clout here. I wasn't even a demon, didn't report through the hierarchy of hell like the others here did. As an independent contractor, I answered only to the big guy. At least, that's how it was originally. Tens of thousands of years had blurred those lines. The very places I'd built and managed had somehow become my full-time job, and I did get called upon now and then to do things that hadn't been in my original contract.

Just in case Eshu was right, I pushed the blueprints aside and got to my feet. It wouldn't hurt to go to this meeting, but it certainly would hurt my paycheck if I refused and found out later there was some weird convoluted logic that made Satan think I was his guy in this matter.

I followed Eshu out of hell and to the human world. He led me to a place called Bob Evans. It was a restaurant where octogenarian humans gathered to have breakfast and talk about the good old days over bottomless cups of coffee. I nodded at a pair of reapers over in a corner booth, who were eating pancakes and watching the room. No doubt two customers were soon to meet their maker.

I'd half expected there to be a private room in the back for this meeting, and was surprised when the server led us to a large table where four angels sat. The two who'd already called dibs on the end chairs glowed with a golden light that indicated they spent a great deal of time in heaven. The other two, who sat next to each other, bore the silvery auras of purgatory.

Everyone had a cup of coffee, but nobody seemed to be drinking it. I gave mine a sniff, then a sip. Eshu pulled out a flask of whisky and added a splash before passing the flask over to me.

"Where is she?" One of the angels was glaring at me, so I supposed the question was also directed toward me.

"Let's start with introductions and the meeting agenda before we get into accusations." One of the purgatory angels said, eyeing the flask with some regret. "I'm Waffa-El, and my associate is Cruici-El. We're both from purgatory."

Eshu snorted and elbowed me so hard I nearly spilled my coffee. "Waffle. They're Waffle and Crucial. Who thinks this shit up?"

"I'm Hades, and this is Eshu. We're both here to represent hell," I said, trying not to laugh. Waffle. Poor guy.

"I'm Remi-El, and this is Zari-El from heaven, and if Mary Jane Hoffman is not returned within the next seven Earth days, we will attack hell and bring her back ourselves."

"Let's not jump to conclusions without hearing all the facts first," Waffle interjected. "All we know is that several souls were missing from each of our areas on the exact same date and time, and that all of those souls have returned except one."

"Mary Jane Hoffman. She went by the nickname Maude

when she was living." Remiel stood. "Return her immediately."

"Why would hell want one of your souls?" I asked. The question really at the top of my mind was why was *I* here and not Lucien?

"Because your numbers are low," Zariel snapped.

Eshu laughed. "Hell's numbers are *so* far from low. They're lined up around the block, waiting for processing. We've had to stack them like cordwood because we've run out of room for all of our souls. Hades is working on an expansion—aren't you?"

I was, but it wasn't because we were bursting at the seams with our current layout. Satan didn't care about crowding damned souls into the punishment areas, but he did care that some of his demons struggled to find adequate housing. I was working on a new section with luxury condos, a racquetball court, and a CrossFit gym. Several of the new arrivals were CrossFit instructors, and we were planning to adjust their scheduled torture so they could run workout sessions for the demons living in the condos.

"Purgatory doesn't have her," Remiel said, pulling my attention back to the topic at hand. "We believe purgatory. We *don't* believe you."

This was ridiculous. "Has anyone asked the souls who vanished and returned what exactly happened to them? Where they were for that brief moment in time? Maybe Mary Jane/Maude Hoffman accidentally got left behind when they came back."

The two angels from heaven glared, but said nothing. Clearly no one had bothered to do any sort of investigation before they started pointing fingers.

"And how *did* the souls vanish?" Cruciel asked. "Hades was the architect for heaven, purgatory, and hell. Perhaps he has some insight into how the souls were able to leave, and reappear."

"He obviously built in escape areas that we're unaware of," Remiel snapped. "We never should have allowed a demon to design heaven. Never."

"I'm not a demon," I told him. "Just because I have some short-term housing in hell and am working on several contracts for them doesn't mean I'm biased. I take all my design projects seriously, and I resent the accusation that I'd build in secret escape areas. Heaven, hell, and purgatory were all built to specification. I did not deviate. I wouldn't. I'm a professional, after all."

Everyone liked to lump me in with Satan and hell, and in all honesty I did do quite a bit of work for the infernal lord. I treated all realms of the afterlife as my own, though. Even the ones that were more fun to visit than to actually live in.

"Then as the divine architect, what is your theory for how the souls were able to escape and return?" Waffle asked.

"A necromancer," I announced.

Silence greeted my words. The only sound was Eshu loudly slurping his coffee.

"There are other ways for souls to escape," I amended. "If a soul has a significant magical ability, they could possibly be able to orchestrate their own jailbreak. There is also some history of bribery, where demon guards have turned the other way, and even facilitated the journey across the river Styx. Some who are particularly gifted among the living have been able to enter the realms of the afterlife and bring a soul back to the living. But this particular occurrence was different."

"Bribery or a sorcerer escaping with his own magic wouldn't don't fit. Not with the escape and return of multiple souls—especially souls in hell, heaven, and purgatory," Zariel mused.

"And heaven's souls do not leave on their own," Remiel added. "No soul in heaven would ever wish to leave."

Eshu snorted at that, but I nodded. Heaven was a lovely place. I should know since I designed it. It might not be *my* cup of tea, but to each his own.

"Why do you think it was a necromancer?" Zariel asked.

"They raise the dead. It's what they do. And raising the dead doesn't just involve animating a corpse either. A powerful necromancer can resurrect. An incredibly powerful necromancer can resurrect more than one person at a time.

"But six of our souls, plus the two from purgatory, plus however many from hell?" Remiel shook his head. "And if this necromancer was powerful enough to resurrect so many, then why return all except one of them an hour later?"

"The return of the souls *is* perplexing," Cruciel said.

"Maybe she picked the one she thought was the best and sent the rest back," Eshu suggested. "I've seen women do that when they go shopping. They'll come home with a dozen dresses that look good on the hanger, try them all on, then take back the eleven they don't want."

"She?" Remiel scoffed. "Necromancers have always been men. If they were women, then they'd be witches and witches can't be necromancers."

Eshu shrugged. "Just because you haven't met a female necromancer, doesn't mean there aren't any around."

"The gender of the necromancer, if this *was* the result of necromantic magic, is moot," Waffle interjected. "And there could be other reasons this happened. Perhaps an astrological alignment caused a weak area in our respective walls."

"Then why did they come back?" I argued, ignoring the implication that my design would have a flaw that was susceptible to a certain astrological alignment. "Those who escape do not often return, unless their magic was faulty, or they violate a condition of the reprieve contract."

Hell had no reprieve contracts, but purgatory did. See? The design specifications were exact.

"And all returned except for one soul?" Waffle looked around at all of us as we nodded in turn. "An additional question might be if there was a reason the missing soul is from heaven, or if that is just a coincidence."

"I still think Satan concocted this whole thing as a cover-up for stealing Maude Hoffman's soul," Remiel countered.

"Why would Satan be interested in that particular soul?" I asked. Angels could get really hung up on certain things, but I got the impression there was more to this woman than her random disappearance from heaven.

"She was a good woman." Remiel puffed out his chest. "Honest. Kind. Humble. Loving to family, friends, and strangers. She also won a blue ribbon at the state fair for her peach crumble."

"Oh, well, no wonder she's in heaven," Eshu commented. "You guys get all the good cooks."

"It might be why Satan was so interested in her," Cruciel added. "Everyone knows he's been wanting to replace his current baker."

If so, there were a whole lot easier ways to do it than to orchestrate a Gordian knot of a cover-up just to steal a soul from heaven. Humans loved bargaining their souls away. Surely there were plenty of skilled chefs willing to make a deal. And if not, Satan could always order delivery. Last I'd heard, Uber Eats delivered to hell.

"Let's formulate an action plan," Waffle clapped his hands and a notepad and pen appeared before him. "We each should question our respective souls as to what happened during their disappearance. Hades can go over the blueprints for our respective areas to make sure there are no flaws that might have caused a mass exodus on that date and time."

I bristled at that, but Waffle continued.

"We should each interrogate those who were in charge of the areas these particular souls resided, as well as determine if there was any lingering trace of outside magic. Shall we reconvene at the same time, four days hence?"

We all nodded, but Remiel continued to glare. "Although we will hold off taking action for now, heaven still considers hell responsible for our missing soul." He shook a finger at me. "Know that if she is harmed in any way, or we find she was stolen and detained against her will, there will be hell to pay."

The others vanished from the room, leaving Eshu and me to drink our spiked coffee.

"I understand that I might need to be at this meeting to vouch for the security of heaven, hell, and purgatory's perimeters, but I really think Lucien or one of the other high-level demons should have attended," I complained. "I'm not really a demon. You're not really a demon. None of these souls are my responsibility."

Eshu shrugged and drained his coffee before reaching for the flask. "True, but you know the structure of every circle and chorus in the afterlife, and you know better than most all the tricky ways souls can be removed, or even leave on their own. All Lucien would have done was get into a fist fight with Remiel over his insults and baseless allegations and slander. You were the better representative to send, demon or no."

I finished my coffee, realizing that he was right. I might not like the extra work, or being thrown into the middle of this, but he was right. I probably was the best contractor for the job.

# CHAPTER 4

## BABYLON

*E*very house on my street was dark as I pulled into my driveway—every house except mine, that is. As I got out of the car, my porch light came on, casting a cheery glow across the lawn. The curtains twitched at the front window, and a gruesome face peered out at me.

"Maude, you can't look out the windows like that. What if the neighbors see you?" I scolded as I came through the door.

She smiled. At least I think she smiled. It was hard to tell since her lips had mummified ages ago, leaving her teeth permanently on display.

"Sssss dark. No one isssss awake. Rrrr you hungry?" Maude gestured to the coffee table where a plate of cheese and crackers sat beside her knitting.

"No thanks," I told her, my stomach uncertain at the thought of eating something the zombie had prepared for me. Thankfully Maude was intimidated by my stove, and convinced my microwave was a product of sorcery, so her attempts to take care of me only extended to snacks she could gather from the pantry and fridge, and crocheting blankets.

When I'd panic-raised a whole graveyard full of the dead to battle demons, Maude had been among those who'd answered my call. But unlike the other dead whose spirits returned to the afterlife once their bodies had shambled back to their graves, Maude had remained behind. I hadn't been able to figure out how to reverse this particular zombie spell, and needed to take her in. That was how I ended up with an undead roommate. It was awkward, but not nearly as awkward as it would have been if my friend Rita's great grandmother was wandering around their family farm.

Maude's body had been in the ground long enough that she should have been just bones, but for some reason she'd partially mummified and retained a tight coating of skin over desiccated tendons and bone. Every now and then a part of her flaked off, or a lock of her long silver hair drifted to the ground, but I'd take that any day over oozing putrification.

"The blanket is coming along nicely," I commented, feeling the need to make conversation with the woman who was clearly lonely here in my house all day by herself.

"My fingerssss are still ssstiff," she complained, spreading them in front of her.

After it had become apparent that Maude would be here until I figured out how to send her back, we'd taken to finding things that might entertain the zombie during my absence. She enjoyed listening to playlists on Spotify and loved daytime television, but it was crochet that she truly enjoyed. There had been a lot of mumbled "darn it" and "oh sugar" at first, but the longer Maude inhabited her dead body, the more movement she seemed capable of. Even her shambling was smoothing out into a more natural gait.

"Well, it looks very nice. I can't wait to curl up under that blanket." After I'd washed it a few times that is, because ew. As it was, I'd probably need to burn the sheets on the guest bed after I managed to either fully resurrect her or send her back. The sheets bothered me enough that I'd opt to buy new ones, but I thought I'd be able to manage using a blanket made by dead hands. As gross as it sounded, I didn't want to hurt Maude's feelings. And honestly it would be kinda cool to have a zombie-crochet blanket. If Maude ever managed to crochet faster and make several of them, I could always give them as Christmas gifts. Or sell them. I was willing to bet an Etsy store with undead blankets would rake in the bucks.

"We arrre going to have a pajama day tomorrrrow?" Maude asked. She was excited about the prospect, although she personally had declined to change out of the drop-waist dress she'd been buried in. For her, the appeal was not so much about a day in lounge attire as it was a television binge and my company.

"I've got to go over the mountain and take care of something for a friend. I'll be gone most of the day, but I'll be back a few hours before I need to go to work. After tomorrow, I've got the Sunday family dinner, and I'll probably need to go back to my friend's place in the evening. I'm not sure if we can have a pajama day this weekend, but we'll definitely watch a few shows in between my running here and there."

Maude smiled, but I could feel the disappointment she was too polite to express. I was disappointed as well. The zombie was surprisingly good company. We liked a lot of the same shows. She didn't eat or drink, so I didn't have to worry about providing party food. Plus, her body had been dead long enough that the only odor was of musty dirt—a smell I was familiar with and actually liked.

"Family and friendsss arrrre important." She waved a bony finger at me. "Sssspend as much time assss you can before you arrre gone."

Maude was all about family, although friends came in a close second. We'd spent a lot of time chatting over the last two weeks and I'd found out that she'd had four children.

She'd outlived two of them as well as her husband, dying at the age of seventy-one. With some quick research, I'd discovered that one more of her children had passed while she was in the grave, but one still lived—Rita's grandmother who was currently in her late seventies. I knew Maude longed to see Bessie, as well as Rita's mom who had been fourteen when Maude had died. It made my heart ache to think of the woman's family, all living within ten miles of us. So close, but they may as well have been a continent away. I could hardly arrange for an introduction to their long dead relative, even if Maude didn't look like an extra from a horror movie.

My own grandmother had died when I'd been an baby. Dad had taken off soon after my birth. Mom hadn't stuck around for much longer. But I had six sisters and a cousin that I was very close to. I understood family. At the very least, I yearned to introduce Maude to Rita so she could bond with one of her descendants and know that her progeny had carried on, but I doubted that reunion would turn out well. Rita would freak at zombie Maude. Not that I blamed her. Even my own sisters found my form of magic icky.

So Maude remained here, cooped up in my house, crocheting, and watching Netflix.

I moved a stack of books off the table, and forced myself to eat a piece of the cheese Maude had put out as a snack for me, just to be polite.

"Do you feel up to trying one of these spells tonight?" I asked her.

When Maude hadn't immediately returned to her afterlife, I'd jumped into research. I'd Googled. I'd e-mailed other witches, asking if they knew any other necromancers I could consult with. I'd ordered more books off eBay than a small-town library. I'd already attempted two spells to try to send

Maude back with no success. Tonight I wanted to try once more.

"Howww about tommmmorrow?" she slurred. "You arrre tired."

She was right. I was tired. Besides, my particular brand of magic didn't need to be worked at night.

"Tomorrow then." I smiled at her and took another piece of cheese from the plate. "I'll see you in the morning."

* * *

AFTER BREAKFAST, I got the spell ingredients ready. Glancing over at Maude, I saw her surrounded by her crochet supplies and flicking through the television channels. She didn't sleep. She didn't eat. The only time she breathed was if she needed to speak. I sucked as a necromancer. Creating a zombie was okay for a quick defense against attacking demons, but I'd sort of resurrected the woman. Only, *not* . I'd half-assed the whole thing instead of actually resurrected her.

I could deal with the ramifications of this if she were in a living body. It would be one thing to teach Maude to live in the modern world, to somehow get her a fake ID and let her live a second life. But this? This was horrible. She was cooped up in my house, decay seemingly suspended but definitely not reversed. I needed to figure out how to return her to the grave, or how to fully resurrect her, because this just wasn't fair to the zombie at all.

Setting the candles on the table, I went to sit beside her and took her bony hand in mine. "Maude, I've never have really asked you this. I honestly don't know if I *can* do anything about your situation, but I'm trying. So far I've been doing spells that would return you to the grave, and I realized I never really asked you what *you* want. Do you want to go back to the grave and whatever afterlife you had? Or do

27

you want me to try to give you a second lifetime as a human?"

She sighed, picking at the sofa cushion with a yellowed nail. "I don't rememberrrrr where I was beforrrre you awakened me. It's fuzzy and unclearrr. I think I was happy, but I don't recall enough to know if I want to go back orrr not. It scarrres me, this not knowing. My situation rrrright now isn't grrreat, but I'm scarrred that the alternative might be worrrse. I mean, at leasssst I'm sorrrrt of alive, rrrright?"

I winced, sad that she knew she was a zombie, and knew she'd never be able to live a normal life like this.

"I'm going to see if I can find someone to help me. Right now, I have three spells that I've found that are supposed to resurrect someone. It's not a lot, but I'm willing to give them a try. I want you to be able to live again if that's your choice, but it may not be possible." I ran a hand through my hair. "Hell, I don't even know if I can even manage to send you back or not. The last spells I performed didn't seem to do squat."

She looked over at me with filmy blue eyes. "It's not yourrrr fault, Babylon."

"Yes, it *is* my fault." I stood and began to pace. "Animating corpses doesn't harm anyone. Bringing back a spirit echo into a dead body doesn't harm anyone. I thought calling for an army of the risen dead to defend my sister and me wouldn't harm anyone either, but it did. It hurt you. It may have also hurt the others I raised that night."

It was the nightmare I didn't want to think about. Were they back in heaven or hell, or were those souls trapped somewhere? The *bodies* had gone back to their graves, but were their *souls* truly at rest, or had I screwed that up as well?

"Everrrry one of us would have come frommm the grave to protect our farm and our family," she told me in a firm tone. "We spent our livesss on that farm. The people that live therrre now are the children of my grandchildren. It wassss my honor to defend them, as well as you and your sssister. And I know the othersss feel the same."

I hoped so.

"I want to do right by you, Maude. And I want to make sure the others are definitely safe and at rest."

"I know you'll do alllll you can, Babylon. And in the meantime, I'll make blanketsss. I promisssse not to prepare any more food, though. After some of my hair fell off in the oatmeal thisss morning, I decided cooking isn't a good idea." She sighed. "It's a shame. I wasss quite a good cook when I was living, you knowww. My baked goods were considered the best arrrround. I even won a blue ribbon for my peach crrrrumble."

For a second I thought about offering to introduce her to Glenda, my foodie chef sister, but I didn't want to freak my family out.

Who was I kidding? I didn't want to let my sisters know that I'd screwed up something so monumentally.

But Maude's situation wasn't going to resolve on its own. I needed help, which meant I was going to have to confess my deeds. And Maude needed to get out and among people other than me. The only place she'd be remotely welcome would be Accident, where supernatural beings felt comfortable walking about in their own skin. But even a town of selkies, shifters, vampires, and more would hesitate to welcome a zombie with open arms.

I needed assistance, but in the meantime, I wanted to try everything I could to help Maude. So I got to work, setting up candles, eyeing the spell I'd marked in one of the books I'd bought off eBay, and gathering my ingredients. When I was ready, I pulled the blackout shades down, drew the curtains, and turned off the television.

"Ready?" I asked Maude.

She smiled and rose. "What sssshould I do?"

"Stand over here by the table," I told her. "Then disrobe. I need to rub some oil into your skin for this spell, and you'll need to be naked."

She hesitated, and I could swear I saw a blush creep up her neck and across her cheeks. "My body doesn't look verrry good." She shook her head and let out a raspy laugh. "It didn't look verrry good at ssseventy-one when they ppput me in the grrround, but it looksss worse now. My ssskin is coming offff, and I'm blotchy and green in placesss. And ssso bony."

I went over to her and gently put a hand on her shoulder. "Maude, I'm a necromancer. I see the dead in various stages of decomposition all the time. Their appearance doesn't bother me. *Your* appearance doesn't bother me. To me you're beautiful."

She nodded and smiled shyly up at me. Then she moved into position and, with nervous fingers, disrobed. I kept my gaze averted as I went about turning the lights off. The house was pitch-black with the special shades and heavy curtains, so I used my cell phone light to find my way in front of Maude. Turning it off, I lit the candles, knowing where they were after years of performing magic at this table.

Then I looked at Maude.

She looked less alarming in the flickering candle light— more like a vampire bride from an old silent movie. I picked up a bottle and poured some of the contents into my hands.

"This is cedar oil. I need to rub it into your skin," I told her.

I proceeded after she nodded in agreement. Her skin was so fragile, and had slipped in some places and flaked in others, so I was very gentle, only brushing the oil on and not actually rubbing it into her skin as the instructions had stipulated. I was pretty sure this spell was meant to be done on a newly dead body and not one quite as decayed as Maude's, but I was hoping it would work anyway.

By the time I was done, the overwhelming smell of cedar had filled the room and Maude glistened in the candle light. I wiped my hands, lit the cone of myrrh, then walked counter-clockwise around the zombie, waving the incense smoke over her from head to toe on all sides of her body.

"Rewind the hand of time. Let bloom once more that which has decayed. Return the dead to the living."

When I stood in front of Maude once more, I reversed directions, waving the incense over her as I circled her clockwise.

"Rewind the hand of time. Let bloom once more that which has decayed. Return the dead to the living."

The smoke blurred my vision, but I squinted against it and took Maude's hands in mine.

"Live. Live. Live," I chanted as I poured my magic into her. The candle flames roared high, then extinguished. I held on to Maude until I felt the spell slip away, then stepped back to turn on the lights.

"Oh my."

I spun around at Maude's soft exclamation, only to have my hopes crushed. Her skin was firmer, her body less skele-tal. She actually had lips to cover her teeth, and eyelids to blink over the milky orbs. The spell had definitely reversed the time of her decomposition, but she was still a corpse. She was still a zombie.

"I'm sorry." Tears stung my eyes. I'd failed at sending her back to the grave, and I'd failed at this. There were more spells I could try, but I was starting to doubt my abilities as well as my power.

"Don't be sorry." She reached out to squeeze my shoulder. "I look so much better. And I can speak clearly now! Babylon, this is amazing."

"It's not amazing." I sniffed. "You're still dead. It failed. I failed."

She held out a hand and looked at her fingers. "This doesn't seem like failure to me. Maybe this is just step one in my resurrection. You worked a miracle, Babylon. And I have faith that eventually you'll be able to resurrect me. And if not, that you'll eventually be able to return me to the grave. The first two spells did nothing at all, but this one…"

She had faith in me. Too bad I was losing faith in myself. But Maude seemed genuinely thrilled with the effects of this spell, even if I was disappointed.

I'd keep trying. I'd keep studying, buying books of eBay, and trying to find a necromancer to help me. I wouldn't give up.

I owed it to Maude to never give up.

# CHAPTER 5

## HADES

"*P*lease have a seat." I motioned the six souls toward the chairs surrounding the huge table. We were in one of hell's conference rooms—the only one I'd been able to reserve on such short notice. It was on the smaller side for the size of the group, but I liked the polished bone table and the leather chairs—artificial human skin, because even Lucifer had to cut a few corners to keep within a budget.

"Now." I tapped my pen against the notepad I'd brought with me. "I've asked all of you here because I'm investigating what happened two weeks ago when you all were summoned out of hell for an hour."

The six souls exchanged looks, their expressions perplexed.

"You." I pointed to a tall, gaunt man who was staring down at the table, and waited until he looked up at me. "What do you remember about that time?"

He reached up and scratched his bald head. "Not much, sir. I was swimming the endless lake of lava when suddenly I was back home. Only it didn't look like it did when I was alive. There was a barn where the milking shed used to be, and a whole field of corn in what used to be the sheep pasture."

I nodded, pleased he'd remembered something even if none of this was particularly helpful.

"Do you know who summoned you?" I asked.

He shook his head. "Could have been anyone. Place was absolute chaos, sir. There was a party with music and tables full of food. People racing around and screaming. Bunch of demons running around a cornfield trying to locate and catch squirrels. All I knew was I needed to defend my farm and my family from the demons, so that's what I did. When the demons were gone, we went back to our graves, and I was suddenly in hell again, swimming in the endless lake of lava."

This had to have been the weirdest story I'd ever heard. Demons didn't just run amok attacking groups of humans anymore. The 1632 treaty of Erebus forbade anything besides one-on-one demonic attacks, except for during certain astrological events. Why would a bunch of demons attack humans having a party? Or be looking for squirrels in a cornfield?

"Does anyone else have additional information?" I'd hoped one of these Hoffman souls would be able to point me straight to the necromancer who'd summoned them so I could retrieve heaven's missing soul and get back to my real job. Those new Cliffs of Despair weren't going to build themselves.

A short, stout woman raised her hand.

"Yes?" I prodded.

"There were zombie animals there fighting the demons along with live animals," she informed me. "I almost stepped on an undead rat. I don't like rats. I don't like them alive, and I don't like them dead."

Okay. Perhaps the demons were targeting the necromancer for some reason, and he needed to pull out all the stops to defend himself. It didn't explain why he'd kept one of the souls, or why the demons were after squirrels, but it was a lead I could possibly follow up on. *Someone* in hell must know about a rogue band of demons who went joyriding to the human world two weeks ago to attack a necromancer and chase squirrels.

"We had to protect the farm," another man spoke up. "And our family. We might be condemned to hell, but we still got standards. If the family calls us to fight demons on the farm, we're gonna be there."

I frowned, wondering about that for a second. Souls just couldn't leave their afterlife to answer the call of their families unless there was magic involved. Was this man implying that a member of his family was the necromancer? If so, then perhaps a quick trip to the human world and the Hoffman family farm would lead me to the missing soul.

The rest of the souls had nothing new to offer, so I dismissed them, giving them the afternoon off from their punishments in thanks for their cooperation. Steve's very thorough report had the address for the Hoffman farm, so I popped down there, hoping that through some miracle, I'd find Maude Hoffman standing by the barn, waiting to be returned to heaven.

Sadly, the only thing I found by the barn was an old tractor and a calico cat who eyed me before sauntering off into the fields.

It was a nice farm. The layout was aesthetically pleasing and practical. I felt the placement of the barn over the previous milk shed and the transformation of the pasture into a cornfield were good choices. The wood-sided farmhouse was weathered, but had a much-loved charm. This was a home—and it had been a home for many, many generations.

I made my way over to the cemetery, keeping one eye on the house in case a resident noticed my trespass and came out to confront me. The family graveyard was surrounded by a short iron fence. Weeds were getting a little out of hand around some of the stones, but it was clear that someone took care of this place. The grass had been trimmed in the last week, and a few of the markers had flowers next to them. I walked up to the one for Mary Ann "Maude" Hoffman and knelt down to straighten the spray of fall mums by the granite stone.

She'd been born in the early part of the twentieth century and died in 1984. Beloved wife and mother. Blue ribbon winner for her peach crumble. Wow, that peach crumble must truly be amazing if it had earned mention on the woman's tombstone.

I stood and walked around the cemetery, noting that none of the graves appeared disturbed—even Maude's. I couldn't feel any residual magic from the spell, but that was no surprise. After two weeks, even the most sensitive individual probably couldn't pick anything up. What was more interesting was that I couldn't feel any current of magic at all in the area of the cemetery or the farm. If there were a necromancer living here, I would have expected them to have worked some magic in the last few weeks that I could find traces of. That meant the person who'd raised all those dead didn't live here. It was either a family member who resided elsewhere, or someone unconnected with the family.

But why would someone unconnected with the family be here that particular night during a party? And care enough about what was going on to exert the incredible amount of magical power it took to raise over a dozen bodies from the grave?

It would be weird to knock on the farmhouse door and ask the residents if anyone in their family or among their friends was a necromancer, and I didn't want to take the risk of lingering long enough to be seen, so I went back to my office in hell and called for Steve to come in. Within seconds of the summons, he was walking through my door.

"What's up boss?" Steve plopped down in a chair and put his feet up on the coffee table.

I glared at him until he removed his feet. "I seem to have been saddled with a project involving those souls who briefly went missing a few weeks back."

He sat up, practically bouncing with excitement. "So my report was useful? I did good?"

"Yes, you did good." The guy was like an eager puppy, but the report had actually come in handy in this instance. "And I need you to do some further digging into the matter. Get me a list of all necromancers currently in hell and where they reside. Then please check with your friend in Purgatory and ask if their two missing souls were able to shed any light on who summoned them. I also want you to ask around and find out who the demons were that attacked the Hoffman farm two weeks ago—it was at the same moment the souls went missing, so it shouldn't be too hard to discover who was out of hell at the time."

Steve's eyes widened. "They're connected? Ooo, Lucifer is not going to like this one bit."

"He probably won't, but no one is going to tell him about it until our investigation is complete and we have a report finalized. Understand?"

Steve nodded, then dashed off to get to work while I got out the designs for the new Cliffs of Despair. I had some suspicions about this whole summoning thing, but I didn't want to divulge anything right now. Call it a gut instinct, but something told me I would be better off keeping all of this quiet for now. Or possibly keeping it quiet forever.

# CHAPTER 6

## BABYLON

*C*rossing the mountain range into Accident always sent a wave of homesickness over me. My house was only half an hour away from home, and I loved living in the human world, but there was a part of me that would always miss this place.

I pulled into town, waving at a group of fairies standing by the front door of the diner as I drove by. Brandy and Ricky were sitting outside the firehouse. Mr. Broadlegs was sweeping the sidewalk in front of his shop. As much as I wanted to swing by and chat with everyone, I had a lot to do today. I needed to go up to Savior Mountain and check out the ghost situation with Clinton and his pack. Then I needed to stop by the law firm to see Cassie and finally confess what I'd done two weeks ago.

But first I was going to get breakfast, and visit the one being in Accident whose former job had to do with the dead and their souls. Nash was a short-order cook in the diner, and he was my sister Ophelia's main squeeze. But before he'd met her and fallen in love, he used to be a reaper.

I pulled around the back of the block and down an alley

that led to a parking lot right behind the diner. A narrow walkway led between two buildings and around to the front. There were still quite a few people inside, even though the breakfast crowd was starting to thin out a bit.

Ducha, a hyena shifter, was dressed in an impeccable navy pantsuit. She sat across from Marcus, a panther shifter, who was our town prosecutor, and my eldest sister's ex-boyfriend. The two shifters worked together, but there was enough icy tension coming off the hyena to power the diner's walk-in fridge. I waved at the rat shifter, Officer Watts, who was dousing his omelet in ketchup, and nodded to our resident chimera, Emma.

Sliding into a booth, I took a look at the menu and placed my order with my waitress, Willow, a sylph who'd gone to school with me.

"Can Nash pop out of the kitchen if he's got a few minutes to take a break?" I asked her.

"Sure." She bobbed slightly, her magic suspending her a few inches above the ground. "We're starting to slow down from the rush anyway."

Nash actually brought my food out to me—fluffy, golden pancakes with sliced strawberries and powdered sugar on top. I ignored the butter and syrup and got in a mouthful before he could slide into the booth opposite me.

Heaven. Pure heaven. The only thing better was Glenda's cooking.

"I've got a reaper question I'm hoping you can help me with," I told him, taking another quick bite of pancake.

"Ask away." Nash smiled and I thought, not for the first time, how lucky my sister was. He was so darned nice. And darned easy on the eyes as well. Many of my sisters liked the edgy guys, or life-of-the-party funny guys. In my opinion, Ophelia had snagged the best of them. Kind. Loving. Considerate. Patient and even tempered. Slim with lean muscle and a cute butt that I was willing to bet looked even better without those pants.

I was a butt girl. So sue me.

I know, I know. Hard to believe that a necromancer with fire-engine-red hair and a zombie roommate would be attracted to this sort of man. Bring on the nerdy guy! The beta dude! Others could keep their alpha assholes for themselves. Me? I liked the men who'd do anything for me, *and* be genuine nice guys as well.

Which, looking back, made me wonder what the hell I'd been doing with Cameron. Jerk. Butt-wipe. Douche Canoe.

Yeah. No. I wasn't going to think about Cameron today. Nope, I was going to think about these amazing pancakes, the ghosts on Savior Mountain, and how to resurrect Maude. Not some jerk who'd ghosted right when I'd thought I'd found the perfect guy.

Pushing thoughts of my disaster of a last relationship away, I got back to why I was here.

"So, here's my question. When you separate a soul from a body and send it to the afterlife, does it ever come back? Or somehow not make it to the afterlife?" I asked as I cut another bite of pancake and pushed it around on my plate.

Nash leaned back in the booth, not one ounce of suspicion on his face. "There is a transition, a journey. If the journey is interrupted, then the soul *could* remain here as a spirit."

"Interrupted? Like they're on their way to heaven, and something happens?"

He shrugged. "It's rare, but the psychopomp that leads them may become untethered from the soul. Usually they're picked up again with only a very short delay. Either another psychopomp grabs them, or a reaper finds them and sends them off once more."

"But what if that didn't happen?" I asked.

"They'll sometimes hover around where they became untethered, or return either to their body or a familiar location from their life. They'll be a ghost until they're found and sent off once more. Some spirits choose not to move on, no matter how hard I urge them, but most are eager to head to the afterlife. And, of course, those destined for hell don't have much of a choice. Hell's minions will seek them out if they don't appear at the gates soon after their demise. A contract is a contract, after all."

"Some return to the body?" I poked again at my pancakes. "Do any of those become zombies?"

"Not without help. Only a necromancer can cause the dead to rise. A soul that returns to its body soon realizes that they've died and leaves. They may haunt the graveyard and the spot where they are buried, but there's no sense in hanging around inside a decomposing, inanimate body."

I ate a few more bites of pancake, working up the nerve to ask my next question.

"Do you know any necromancers?"

"Besides you?" he smiled. "No. Necromancers are very rare, and I'm sure you can understand why they may not want to hang around reapers who are duty bound to take the souls they may be trying to resurrect."

"Animation doesn't require a soul," I reminded him.

"No, and the zombies necromancers create use no more than an echo or shadow of the soul. I may not have known them, but I've heard of ones who can pull souls from the afterlife and use them to give their zombies intelligence and sentience. Those necromancers have the power to resurrect, which is something heaven and hell both frown upon."

His words caused that pancake to sit like a lump in my stomach.

"I don't know how to do that. I've never had a teacher. None of our ancestors's spell books have anything to do with necromancy. I'm on my own here, and sometimes that means I don't really know what I'm doing. It's hard. If I…screw up, then there's no one to turn to for advice."

He reached out and patted my hand. "Do you want me to ask around, Babylon? Ask some of the other reapers if they know of any living necromancers who I could put you in touch with?"

I nodded. "I need help, Nash. My sisters don't understand what I do. No one understands what I do. You're probably the only one I know who sorta does." I took a deep breath, then went on. "I did something. I did it for the right reasons, and I tried to fix things, but nothing I do seems to be working. I need help. All the people I'd normally go to for help can't assist me. And they'd probably be horrified and wigged out at what I've done."

"Your sisters love you," he assured me. "They might be a bit nauseated at some of the magic you do, but that doesn't mean they won't understand and try to help. They know you're a good person, a good witch. Your powers are just… odd compared to theirs."

I nodded, realizing he was right. "If you could help me find a necromancer, that would be wonderful. And in the meantime, do you think you could possibly take a look at someone and give me your professional reaper opinion?"

"I'm not a reaper anymore, but you know I'll do anything I can to help you, Babylon. You're Ophelia's sister. That makes you my sister, too."

"You don't have any brothers, do you?" I asked, thinking once more about how lucky Ophelia was.

He shot me a quizzical look. "Reapers don't have siblings."

"Never mind." I waved the comment away. "I haven't told anyone else this. I'm not asking you to keep it from Ophelia or anyone, but if you could possibly hold off until I let Cassie know this afternoon before mentioning it, I'd appreciate it."

He made a lips-zipped motion that had me cracking up. "I keep no secrets from Ophelia, but other than her, I won't tell a soul."

That would do. I took another deep breath and let it out, working up the nerve to confess. "Two weeks ago I animated some human dead from a family graveyard to protect Addy, me, and a group of humans from the demons that were attacking us. I panicked and evidently pulled entire souls from their afterlife. When I returned them to the grave, one didn't go back."

Nash looked confused. "You resurrected a group? Then killed them all off except one."

"I didn't kill them off!" Yikes, how could he think that about me. "And I didn't resurrect them. I created zombies, but instead of pulling only an echo of their souls, I accidentally pulled the entire soul."

"You took a complete soul from the afterlife and put it into a non-resurrected, corpse body?"

I didn't like that worried frown on Nash's face. "Yes. I didn't realize it at the time. We were fighting, and the zombies were doing their thing. At the end, I dismissed them, and they all went back to their graves except one."

"Are you sure they went back to their graves?"

My stomach twisted with horror at the thought of souls housed in corpses, basically buried alive in the dirt. "I checked. As soon as I saw that Maude was still walking around, I checked the other corpses. There is not even a whisper of life in them. They're just bodies. But I don't know how to make sure the souls went back to their afterlife and aren't just floating around somewhere. And I don't know what to do about Maude."

Nash ran a hand through his hair. "Can you sense spirits? Sense their ghosts? You should be able to do that with your necromantic magic."

I nodded. "Yes. I checked the area by the graves and there were only the usual echos. I even walked around the farm and the house. If their souls had remained, I feel certain they would have hung around the grave, or at least the farm where they lived their lives."

Thankfully, I needed both a sigil and an incantation to open my third eye to the spirit world, because going through life aware of every ghost and specter would be difficult. Wraiths and poltergeists were visible without conscious use of magic, but the little wisps of spirits that filled our world remained hidden from me until I wished to see them.

"That's good." Nash drummed his fingers on the table. "If their souls were somewhere in transit or floating about the veil, other reapers and psychopomps should be able to sense them. I'll double check with my contacts, but the good news is that if you failed to return them to their afterlife and they're not still here as ghosts, then they were probably picked up and taken to the appropriate place."

I let out a relieved breath. I'd been so worried. Now I could focus my attention on Maude. Coming to Nash had been the right idea. If he could assure me that the other souls weren't somewhere lost in transit, it would do a lot for the gnawing anxiety that had worried me over the last few weeks.

"What are you going to do about the soul that remained behind?" Nash winced. "In a dead body?"

I ran a hand through my hair. "I was hoping you'd have some ideas on that. I tried two different spells to send her back to the afterlife, and both failed. This morning I tried a spell to resurrect her. Her body definitely looks better, but it's still dead. So although the spell failed, I think I'm on the right track."

"That's good to hear." He tilted his head. "I wonder why

the dismissal spells didn't work? I'd think those would be easier than the resurrection ones."

I'd given that some thought on the way over. "I talked to Maude this morning, and she wants to stay. She doesn't remember the afterlife, and she truly wants a second go around. She wants to see her family and live again. I don't think I'm a strong enough necromancer to overpower her wishes—even though she hadn't voiced them until this morning."

He nodded. "That's possible. I'll ask around to see if there is a necromancer who has successfully resurrected someone that you can speak to. Otherwise, I'd suggest you just keep trying. You're more powerful than you realize, Babylon. It may take you some time, but I believe you'll succeed."

I wasn't sure how much time I had, though. Being a zombie had seemed to halt Maude's decay, but how long would she be happy hanging out in my house, unable to see anyone or go anywhere?

"Thank you." I told Nash with heartfelt sincerity. It felt good to let someone know what I'd done, and to have some reassurance that I was on the right track.

And I was definitely going to tell Cassie this afternoon. But in the meantime, I had a group of werewolves to visit.

Nash returned to the kitchen, leaving me to finish my pancakes. I paid, gave a quick wave to the other customers, then headed out to Savior Mountain.

# CHAPTER 7

## BABYLON

The main road up Savior Mountain nearly killed my car's suspension. The werewolves had done a great job at clearing away downed trees and rocks, but heavy fall rains had created potholes that made driving to their compound like navigating an obstacle course.

I slowly made my way past a stand of spruce and saw movement to my left. One wolf dashed ahead to herald my arrival, while another moved to slowly jog beside me as I drove on. Finally I saw the compound ahead. Among the dozens of buildings, half were unpainted, some of them wrapped in tar paper to guard against the approaching winter weather. What would be neat yards and gardens come spring were now only patches of dirt and mud. Smoke curled from several of the homes, and the tantalizing smell of smoked meat tickled my nose. I parked where my wolf escort indicated and made my way on foot to the lodge that the alpha called home.

Clinton had built a very nice settlement on Heartbreak Mountain when he'd been trying to wrestle a portion of the existing werewolf pack territory away from his father to form his own pack. It had been a shame he'd had to leave it behind, but Clinton's father, Dallas, had contributed money, materials, and labor to compensate the new pack for the loss. In the end, this arrangement would suit the werewolves better. Distance and distinct territory lines would hopefully stave off fighting between the two packs, and the establishment of a common hunting area on Heartbreak Mountain should give both groups a sense of shared community.

But that was all wishing on our part. Ultimately, the success of this pack would be on their shoulders, and all we witches could do was help whenever needed.

A few of the other werewolves came to the doors of their homes to watch me approach. My escort stayed by my side all the way to the lodge door. Living my whole life among shifters meant I recognized his presence as a courtesy, an honor. There were times when an escort meant distrust. I'm not sure how to explain how I knew the difference between the two, but I did.

Clinton met me at the door and ushered me inside. Three other werewolves sat around a huge table.

"This is Justelle, Bay, and Flick," Clinton introduced the wolves who nodded in turn. "Each one of them has had an experience during the last few weeks with what they feel is a ghost."

I sat down across from them and smiled reassuringly. It couldn't have been easy for any of them to come forward like this. Werewolves hated anything to do with spirits and the undead. Many of them still crossed the road when they saw a vampire or a wraith coming. They probably would have all had a collective stroke if I'd arrived with Maude in tow.

"Lots of us in the pack have had things fall off shelves, or felt a cold spot, or the sensation of something touching us when nothing's there," Justelle explained. "Most just chalk it up to a natural occurrence—a shelf not being completely level, a draft, spider webs. But what I saw…I just can't explain it."

I took a notepad and a pen out of my bag. My memory was good, but people seemed to be reassured when you took notes, like you were really listening and taking their claims seriously.

Clinton sat at the end of the table. "Flick, you go ahead and tell Babylon what happened."

The werewolf eyed me nervously. She looked young, not more than twenty, but werewolves aged slowly and she was probably closer to thirty. Flick was pretty with soft ashy brown hair in a high ponytail, big dark eyes, and a host of freckles scattered across her nose and cheekbones. The soft fur of a blonde beard lined her jaw. Werewolves were furry. It was common—and considered attractive—for even the women to have facial hair.

"I was out at night for a walk." Flick glanced apologetically over at Clinton. "My guard shift was done at midnight, and I can never sleep right away."

Clinton nodded for her to go on.

"There's a bunch of sugar maples about a quarter mile or so from the compound. One came down a few weeks ago during a storm and blocked the road. It's a big stand of trees, all of them really old and thick with a broad canopy. I love to lay in the moss among the roots and look up at the moonlight streaming through the leaves in a pattern like lace."

That was downright inspirational. Werewolves had a reputation as practical, physical, hot-tempered, but once you got to know them you realized there were just as many sculptors and singers as any in any other group. Flick might serve her guard duty, but I'd be willing to bet she painted or wrote poetry in her free time.

"Anyway," the werewolf continued. "That's what I was doing

when I saw the ghost. It was this filmy white thing, and at first I thought it was a small patch of ground fog. It came from one of the trees, coalesced into a bipedal shape, then glowed with an inner light. I still thought it was fog, or some of that bioluminescent fungus, because there's no such thing as ghosts."

"I can assure you there are," I said.

Flick eyed me apologetically. "Well, I've never seen any before. And no one I know has either. So I didn't think it was a ghost until it got close to me. It was like a person made of light and fog, except it was kinda blurry, so I couldn't see if it was a human or what. There was no smell to it either. The air got really cold when it came close."

"How cold?" Shifters tended to think anything above freezing was warm, so I was assuming the air temperature must have dropped thirty degrees or so.

"It was around forty degrees that night, and laying there it suddenly dropped down close to zero." Flick shivered and rubbed her arms. "It reached out to me and said I needed to help find some tinsel, or something like that."

"Tinsel?" I asked, wondering if she'd misheard. Ghosts didn't often speak, and those who could often garbled or slurred their words.

"I *think* that's what it said." Flick shook her head. "That can't be right, though. Why would a ghost coming out of a maple tree in the middle of a forest want Christmas decorations?"

"Yeah. If it had been a pine tree, I could have maybe seen it," Justelle chimed in. "That's a tree you put tinsel on, not a sugar maple."

"What happened next?" I asked Flick.

"I ran like my tail was on fire, that's what happened next," she retorted. "No way was I gonna lay around and let some ghost freeze me into a block of ice, or stuff me into a tree or something. I got the heck out of there, got home, and hid under my covers until daylight."

Normally such a confession would have had the other werewolves jeering and calling Flick a coward, but all of them, including Clinton, listened to her story with wide-eyes.

"Have you experienced anything similar since then?" I asked.

Flick shook her head. "No, but I haven't been back there. It was my favorite place, but now I'm scared to go."

"Clinton mentioned some of the others had things knocked off their shelves, cold spots in their houses, stuff like that. Has any of that been happening to you, Flick?" I asked.

Ghosts concentrated around a strand of maples would lead me in a different direction of thought than ghosts who were trying to get the attention of the shifters on the mountain, regardless of where on the mountain they were.

"Well, yeah. But that stuff is kinda normal, you know?" Flick shifted in her seat. "Foggy people asking for Christmas decorations isn't normal."

True.

"Justelle, you go next," Clinton prompted.

Justelle looked about five years or so younger than Flick. Her honey blonde hair was done up in an intricate braid. The light fuzz along her jawline would turn into soft fur as she got older.

"I live at the north end of the compound with my two brothers. We've had a persistent cold spot at the far west corner of our house for the last two months." She gave me a tentative smile. "We thought it was some weird geologic thing, although my younger brother insists we must have built the house over a grave."

"We didn't come across any bones when we excavated for

the compound," Clinton jumped in. "If we had, I'd have stopped construction and called you right away."

Werewolves were very superstitious about disturbing the dead. Dallas had sent for me three years ago when they'd accidentally unearthed a satyr grave when digging for a smoke pit. The incident had involved ceremonies and sacrifices as well as my contacting the deceased satyr to ask for his forgiveness in the disturbance of his remains. The werewolves marked the ground as consecrated and dug their smoke pit elsewhere. To this day they gave the location the same fearful respect they gave their own cemeteries, even though the deceased satyr hadn't seemed to care about the fire pit one way or the other.

Justelle nodded at Clinton's statement. "Anyway, when Flick told me what happened to her, I thought maybe the ghost she saw was a dryad or an ent or something, so I went out the next night. There was a silvery sort of ground fog all around the trees. It didn't get cold or anything, and I didn't see anything that looked like a person, but that fog sure was creepy."

"Creepy how?" I asked, thinking how odd it was for a werewolf to admit anything was creepy.

"The fog came closer until I could hardly see anything through it. Then I got this tingly feeling like hands were touching my arms, like they were trying to tug on me and pull me somewhere, but they didn't have the strength. I heard whispers but couldn't tell what they were saying. Once the whispers started, I left. The fog cleared the moment I was free of that grove of trees. It was a clear night with a bright quarter moon. Not a cloud in the sky. I've seen ground fog before, but there wasn't any down by the stream or in the valley, just in that cluster of sugar maples."

I nodded, made a few notes on my pad of paper, then turned to Bay.

The male werewolf was built like a lumberjack. He was so furry that I doubted he did more than change physical shape when he shifted into his wolf form. Thick wavy facial hair stood out a good six inches from his cheeks. It was so long it completely covered his mouth. When he spoke, all I could see was the movement of his bushy beard.

"I chop trees for the compound. Sometimes it's firewood. Sometimes it's wood for the meat smokers. Sometimes it's for the carpentry and furniture making crews. A few days ago late at night I heard some noises out back of my house where I keep the wood until the other crews come to get it. I went out, thinking maybe an animal was out there or something. There was no animal, but a tree I took down for the carpentry crew was bleeding."

I paused my notes to look up at him in shock. "Bleeding?"

He nodded, his eyes wide. "I saw it. And I smelled it. Wasn't sap or nothing. It was blood."

"What sort of blood?" Werewolves had incredible noses. If Bay smelled blood, he should have been able to smell what the blood was from. In detail. As in "it was a fifteen-year-old female black bear shifter with a urinary tract infection who'd eaten a blueberry muffin for breakfast" detail.

"I don't know. I've never smelled that sort of blood before." He wrinkled his nose. "There was something wrong with it, though. And it smelled like magic—like bad magic."

Magic smelled? That was the first I'd ever heard of that.

"Witch magic? Did it smell similar to magic that I or any of my sisters do?"

Bay frowned and looked down at the table. A few seconds passed before he raised his head. "No. Maybe a little like Sylvie's magic, but not the same. And it wasn't human or witch blood."

Blood from a being that Bay hadn't ever encountered

before—a being who either had magic, or had been exposed to magic.

"Bay doesn't go into town much, but with the building going on up here and everyone helping, he's met most of the folks calling Accident home," Clinton assured me.

That made what the werewolf had said even more of a mystery. Lots of the wolf shifters went their whole lives without seeing more than a handful of those outside of their compound. Those wolves wouldn't know what a minotaur or a troll or a vampire smelled like. But Clinton was right. All of the town had pitched in to help build this community up on Savior Mountain, and the werewolves here would know what they all smelled like—even if they'd never actually seen them face-to-face.

That meant whatever bled on Bay's wood pile was a supernatural being that didn't currently reside in Accident.

"There's more," Bay said ominously. "That wood that was bleeding? It was sugar maple. I took that tree that had fallen and blocked the road a few weeks back, and hauled it over to my house. Nice thick trunk. Straight and true. Would have made good cabinets or flooring."

"Where is this wood now?" I asked.

"Over at the carpenter's place. He put it aside. Clinton said we wouldn't want to cut it up until we'd talked to you."

I put my notepad and pencil back in my bag and stood. "Let's start there."

I followed the four werewolves outside and over to a tidy cabin on the outskirts of the compound. Hand tools were lined up on benches. Planed boards were on saw horses. A tall, thin werewolf with bushy iron-gray hair was sharpening a bladed tool on a leather strop. He glanced up, then stood as we approached, lowering his eyes and giving Clinton a respectful nod.

"Fists, this is Babylon Perkins," Clinton told him. "She wants to see the tree trunk that Bay brought over."

Fists sent me a quick glance, then waved me over to where a thick log lay on a bed of leaves. "This is it. Here's the blood."

I knelt down, noting the red stains on the bark. The tree wasn't actively bleeding anymore. "Bay, are you sure it was actually the tree that was bleeding? Could some animal or something else have been injured and left the blood on the bark?"

"It was bleeding," Bay insisted. "I saw it oozing out of the tree. Scared the heck out of me."

"No doubt." I pulled a penknife and a bag out, scraped some of the blood off the tree trunk, and stored it away for later. These werewolves were scared enough. They didn't need to have to witness my freaky magic on top of a haunting and a bleeding tree.

As the werewolves watched, I went over the tree from top to bottom, looking for anything that might give me a clue, like sigils carved in the bark. Near the bottom of the tree, I saw a discolored and jagged section.

"What happened here?" I asked Bay. He'd said the tree had fallen in a storm and blocked the access road, but the werewolf had clearly trimmed the ends of the log. I wondered why he hadn't cut this damaged section off as well before hauling it in to the compound.

"That broke off after I brought the log in," Bay explained. "There's a little hollow part there in the wood that I didn't see when I was trimming the ends. I figured Fists would work around it when he was planning the wood."

I picked up a curved knife from the table and inserted the blade into the place where Bay had indicated the hollow part was. Sure enough, the blade sunk into the wood nearly to the handle before hitting something solid.

"You want me to cut that bad portion out so you can see it better?" Fists asked.

I hesitated, because cutting into a tree that might have an enchantment on the wood might not be a wise thing to do— at least, not a wise thing for a *werewolf* to do.

Digging some chalk, a bundle of sage, and a handful of stones out of my bag, I motioned for the werewolves to step back. My magic was necromancy. Normally sigils of protection and safety were more powerful when they were done by my other sisters, but when it came to guarding against the undead or the spirit world, my sigils were just as potent.

Since I didn't know what I was dealing with, and I was concerned for the safety of the werewolves in the compound, I drew my protective circle around the entire tree trunk. With the tiny nub of chalk left, I drew additional symbols around the blood stains and where I assumed the hollow portion was.

"What's the grass bundle for?" Flick asked, eyeing the sage with curiosity.

"It's for afterward," I told her. "Once I'm done here, I'll smudge the area just to make sure no harmful energy remains. It's an extra precaution."

All five werewolves let out a long breath at that. They were trusting me to keep them safe, to take care of this problem. The thought made me proud. Me, the weird dead-thing witch, was helping them. It was a rare occasion to show some of the residents of Accident that my magic wasn't something to be feared, and that I could play just as much of a part in the community as my sisters.

"And the stones?" Clinton asked.

"To attract the spirit I suspect is trapped in this wood."

They all tensed back up at that, and I sighed, my pride short-lived.

"I need to bring the spirit who has been haunting you to me if I'm going to try to convince him to leave," I explained.

The werewolves nodded, but took a few extra steps back. Knowing they weren't going to like what I was about to do, I turned to block their view and began placing the stones. Red jasper. Hematite. Tiger's-eye. Rose quartz.

Then with a whispered incantation, I plunged the curved blade of the knife into the tree, through the bark into the hollow space.

The tree screamed, blood welling up around the knife blade. I'd never seen werewolves move so fast in my life. One second they were there, the next they were gone. Although to Clinton's credit, the alpha did carefully make his way back to stand about twenty feet away from the outer edge of the protective circle.

Three shadowy forms materialized around the tree. They were humanoid, and about three feet tall.

*Tinsel.*

I wasn't sure if the word had been spoken, or telepathically communicated, but I'd heard it distinctly. Instead of responding, I pulled the knife from the tree trunk, pushing one of my fingers in through the hole the blade had made. There was something sharp in the hollow, something that vibrated with magic. I widened the hole with the knife enough to get my index finger and my thumb in. The whole time the tree screamed and bled.

A quick glance told me Clinton was still there, ashen as the ghosts in front of me, his hands balled into fists by his sides. Poor guy was probably regretting being the alpha right now. No doubt he desperately wanted to run to wherever the others had gone to hide.

*Tinsel*, the specters moaned.

I groped around in the hollow section, my fingers slick with blood. Finally, I managed to grip the sharp object and ease it out of the tree. Wiping it off on a small towel, I held it up.

Bone. A bone that was an awful lot like the one my sister Addy had brought me a few weeks ago. She said she'd found it near one of the downed trees that had been blocking the access road to the Savior Mountain werewolf compound. I'd stuck it in a jar at home because we'd been rather busy dealing with attacking demons, then I'd been rather busy trying to figure out what to do with Maude. But now I remembered it and knew it was no coincidence that she'd found a bone right next to this tree.

I realized right then that there was a body entombed in this tree. A curse. A horrible, horrible curse that I suspected involved more than the three ghosts in front of me and whoever was trapped in this tree.

Once more, I was in over my head. First Maude with her not-alive/not-dead zombie status and my inability to rectify that situation. Now a major curse, the like of which I'd never seen before. How many were trapped under this spell? And for how long had they suffered?

What did I need to do to release the curse and set them free?

*Tinsel*, the spirits reminded me.

"I know. And I will do everything in my power to help you," I told them. "But this isn't something that can be done with a bundle of sage and a few stones. I need to know the nature of the curse. I need to do some research, to find out how to release all of you from this prison. It might take time, but I won't rest until the curse is broken and you're all set free."

*Tinsel*, they sighed. Then the ghosts vanished, and the blood on the tree dried into the bark. The chalk runes puffed out in a burst of white smoke.

I carefully bagged the bone, then put away the stones I'd not been able to use.

And I burned the sage—more to make the werewolves feel better than for any real protection. They wouldn't need protection from the ghosts haunting them. And no amount of sage was going to put those ghosts to rest.

# CHAPTER 8

## BABYLON

"I'm moving," Bay announced. "No offense to you, Clinton, but I'm going back to Dallas's pack. There's no way I'm going to live in a haunted compound. No way."

"It won't be haunted for long," I tried to assure him and the others. "These are not harmful ghosts. I sense no ill intent from them. They're trapped. I have every intention of releasing them, but it's just going to take some time. Please be patient, and soon enough your compound will no longer be haunted."

"Can we burn the log? Put some of those squiggly chalk marks around the entire compound? Burn more sage?" Clinton asked.

I could see the whole thing had frightened him just as much as it had his pack, but he was the alpha. He needed to put on a brave face and do all he could to solve the problem and keep his people safe.

"I wish it were that simple." I motioned toward the log. "Burning the log won't help, and it might just make things worse. The sigils and sage will keep the spirits from entering

59

the compound, but the pack still needs to come and go. I don't have enough chalk and sage to secure the whole mountain, and I doubt that would even work. There is a curse that keeps the spirits here, and until I can break the curse, I can't send the ghosts elsewhere. They're stuck."

"Let's just get them their tinsel," Justelle proposed. "We'll run into town, buy up all the Christmas stuff we can find, then lay it out in an offering. Then maybe the ghosts will stay away."

"The ghosts won't harm any of you," I repeated. I knew that no amount of reassurance would quell their fears. They were all superstitious, and even benign ghosts were terrifying to them. "Besides," I added. "The tinsel the ghosts are talking about isn't a thing, it's a he. Or she. I'm almost positive that the spirits haunting the compound are the ghosts of the elves who used to live on Savior Mountain. Tinsel is the name of one of the elves."

I wasn't sure if Tinsel was the elf trapped in the log or not, but I knew that the key to breaking this curse and setting the spirits free was in finding out who Tinsel was and what the elf had to do with the curse.

"The elves?" Clinton frowned. "But they left a couple of decades ago. No one's really sure when they went away since they were kinda private-like up here on the mountain. I remember Dad saying one day they were here, and the next day there was nothing but empty houses. Everyone just figured they went back to their fairyland, or elfland, or whatever. It's not like they socialized at all with the others, anyway."

Neither did the werewolves up until recently. Still, I understood what Clinton was saying. The fae races in Accident were very different, but the one thing they had in common was a strange feeling of "other" about them. Most of them owned shops, came to town events, hung out at the bar and sang karaoke with the rest of us. But they still seemed a bit odd compared to the other supernatural residents.

"I'm going to help you, and help the spirits haunting Savior Mountain," I vowed. "But it isn't something that's going to be resolved today. Please stay and have faith in me—have faith that I can take care of this. Don't abandon all you've worked for. Don't abandon your new pack over this. The ghosts won't hurt you. I'm asking you all to stay put, to trust in me."

The five werewolves glanced at each other, then looked to Clinton. The pack alpha regarded me solemnly, then nodded.

"We wolves came to Accident centuries ago, trusting that the Perkins witches would keep us safe. Under their protection, we've been able to honor our culture, maintain our pack, and live our lives openly and as we wished. The Perkins witches are the guardians of Accident, and they have always kept their word. I trust that Babylon Perkins will break the curse and free the spirits so they may move on to their afterlife. Our pack will remain here, and we will do anything we can to aid you in removing the ghosts who haunt Savior Mountain and our compound."

I nodded in return, acknowledging the faith Clinton had in me and the importance of my task.

I couldn't fail—not the werewolves who now called Savior Mountain their home, nor the elves who'd once lived here.

* * *

"ELVES?" Cassie shook her head in disbelief.

I'd caught my eldest sister just as she was returning home from picking up groceries, pulling into the driveway right behind her car. I'd explained the situation with Clinton's pack as I helped her carry in the bags, noting the particularly huge quantity of pork ribs filling several of them. Sunday family dinner had grown with the inclusion of the demon boyfriends of my sisters. That meant a whole lot more food, and quite a crowd at what we'd originally believed to be a huge dining table. Now, that table wasn't quite big enough. Cassie had been insisting some of us eat in the kitchen, like the "kids' table" at Thanksgiving.

I often ended up at that kids' table. Not just because I was the youngest, but because I was the only one in the family still single. Besides our cousin, Aaron, that is.

"Do you know anything about them?" I asked her, meaning the elves. "Did Mom ever mention them? Or Grandma?"

My chest felt tight. I rubbed it, thinking it was a particularly bad time for me to dwell on all the things that burdened my heart.

I had no love-of-my-life, when all my sisters were happily coupled. I had creepy magic that no one really understood, and that weirded out even my own family. Dad had left right after I was born, abandoning us all. Mom ditched us soon after. Even Grandma had died when I was young, leaving Cassie to raise me.

It's like I was some sort of pariah, like I didn't belong even here in Accident where *everyone* belonged. It didn't help that Cameron, my last boyfriend, had up and vanished on me, not even bothering to return my calls. I'd thought we were in love, but clearly I'd been wrong.

Looking back, there had probably been red flags that my unconscious mind had picked up on. We'd dated for months, but I'd never introduced him to my family. Heck, I'd never even mentioned him to my family. Deep down, I must have known something was wrong.

Everything I did seemed to fall apart. My parents. My love life. Maude.

I needed to help Clinton and the werewolves, and the cursed elves. Freeing them would give me a sense of purpose, a feeling of legitimacy. I'd be able to take my place as one of the guardian witches of this town, even though I had icky magic. Even though I would probably spend my life alone, surrounded by animated dead rodents. Even though I was convinced I was the reason our parents had walked out on us. Maybe if I helped the werewolves I'd feel as if I belonged here, as if I were truly part of this family and not some misfortune, some freak of nature.

"I don't remember Mom ever mentioning the elves." Cassie broke into my reverie with her words. "Grandma mentioned them a couple of times, but nothing specific. They'd left when I was really young. I got the impression from what Grandma said that they kept to themselves—even more so than the werewolves. When they vanished, everyone just assumed they returned to their homeland."

"Maybe there's something in the journals?" I suggested.

The attic was filled with the spell books and journals of our ancestor witches. Going through them wouldn't be a quick task, but perhaps we could narrow our search to a specific timeframe and only need to read a dozen journals instead of all of them.

"If you want to go through a few today, you're welcome to go on up to the attic," Cassie replied. "Or you can wait until tomorrow after dinner and we'll help you."

Seven witches' hands would make quicker work of it. "Tomorrow is fine. Maybe I'll come early for dinner to look at them. Do you think the fairies in town might know anything about the elves?"

Some of our fairy residents had been here for over a century. They were distant kin to the elves. Surely a few of them would at least know what, or who, might have caused the curse.

"Ask Mirabelle," Cassie suggested. "She's lived in Accident on and off since Temperance Perkins founded the town. If anyone knows about the elves, it will be her."

Mirabelle owned Mirabelle's Jewelry. I made a note to swing by the store tomorrow as well.

"And talk to Sylvie," Cassie added. "She knows more about curses than any of us."

Our sister Sylvie was gifted with the magic of charms as well as curses, although she never discussed the darker side of her abilities. She might be able to give me some insight on what sort of curse had trapped the elves on Savior Mountain, and what I might be able to do to break it.

"I'll do that," I promised. "And thanks for your help. I want to free these spirits as soon as possible. The werewolves are completely freaked out. They're making noises about ditching the compound and rejoining Dallas's pack if I can't get the ghosts to leave the Mountain."

Cassie grimaced. "Then we'd be right back where we started."

We'd have one werewolf pack with opposing philosophies and increasing tension. Fights. War. And all the effort the folks of Accident had made to support the new splinter pack and peace among the wolves would be for nothing.

"I've got this," I told her, feeling the pressure and worried that I absolutely did not have this. It wasn't the first time. And that thought brought me to the second reason I was here to see Cassie.

"There's...a problem I need to talk to you about." I motioned for Cassie to sit. Her eyes narrowed as she sank into one of the kitchen chairs. "Remember when those demons attacked Addy and me at that bonfire party?"

She nodded, the air crackling with magic. Sparks lit her

brown eyes, telling me my sister was a hair away from lighting the kitchen table on fire. Cassie had been furious that demons had attacked two of her family. She'd gone straight to Lucien, her main squeeze and the son of Lucifer himself, and informed him that the next time a denizen of hell attacked one of her sisters, she was going to personally incinerate him. I didn't know if regular fire could harm a demon, but I was pretty sure Cassie's magic was more like a nuclear crematorium than the flames I'd roasted marshmallows over this past summer. Either way, Lucien had taken Cassie's threat seriously and gone to his father.

Lucifer did what Lucifer wanted, regardless of what his heir demanded, but I got the impression he approved of this union between his son and the most powerful Perkins witch in centuries, and that he was hoping for some future grandbabies. So he'd intervened, and between his influence and some negotiating between the demons, the issue was resolved without anyone being set on fire.

Cassie took a deep breath and dialed down the magic a bit. "Sorry about that. What were you saying about the demons that attacked you and Addy?"

I also took a deep breath, feeling as if I were about to confess something to a parent—because that's pretty much what Cassie was to me. A mother and father all rolled up into one, even though she'd still been a teenager herself when she'd been thrust into that role.

"I animated some dead to defend us." I winced, then amended my statement. "Well, actually I didn't animate them. I needed them to think for themselves because I was too busy to actively pilot all of them and fight off demons myself."

Cassie nodded. "Zombies. I don't normally approve, but it was absolutely justified in this instance. There's no harm in raising zombie insects, rodents, and birds when you're defending yourself and your sister."

Ugh, I so didn't want to tell her this, but I needed help. And although Nash might come through for me, I couldn't continue to keep this from Cassie.

"It wasn't just zombie insects, rodents, and birds," I confessed. "There was a graveyard on the farm. I raised the human dead to help us."

Cassie's eyes widened. "Zombie...people?"

"I panicked," I told her, knowing that was a shitty excuse for going into the gray area of my necromantic magic. "It wasn't just Addy and myself at risk, it was all the humans at the party. And when the fight was over and we were safe, I returned the dead to their eternal rest. I freed their souls to the afterlife and sent their bodies back to their graves."

She nodded, her eyes still wide. "I understand. I might have done the same if...well, if I'd had your sort of magic. It's okay—but don't do it again. There's nothing to be worried about, as long as all the zombies were returned to the grave and their souls to their afterlife."

I winced. "They all were returned to the grave except one. I tried, Cassie. I really tried. And no one was more shocked than I was when she showed up at my door. I mean, I'm glad she showed up at my door rather than freaking out her great granddaughter or some random person at Burger King or something. But I don't know what to do. I've tried twice to send her back and nothing happened. This morning I tried to resurrect her, and it didn't work either. I mean, her body looks better, but it's still dead."

Cassie's eyebrows twisted upward. "What are you saying? There's still a zombie human walking around? One got missed somehow when you sent them back?"

"Yes. She's at my house. And I've been trying to fix it for two weeks. I need help Cassie."

"I'll say you need help," she snapped. "How the hell did this happen?"

"I don't know," I snapped back, distraught over the situation but a bit relieved over finally letting Cassie know about the zombie in my house. "I don't know what went wrong. I mean, I've never raised a bunch of human zombies before, so maybe I just screwed up and missed one when I was sending them back, or screwed up on her summoning. Maybe there was something different about Maude that made her remain behind. Maybe...I don't know Cassie. I never had anyone to help me learn my magic. None of the spell books or journals in the attic have anything about necromancy in them. I don't know any other necromancers. I don't know why Maude is still here, or what to do about it. It's not like I did this on purpose. I didn't mean to, and I'm doing everything I can to fix it, but I need help."

Cassie stood and began to pace. "Okay, okay. Let's both calm down and think through this. You've got a zombie living in your home. And no one else knows or saw her, right?"

I nodded. "Maude is her name. She stays in my house, watching TV and crocheting. She's actually very nice."

"She's not craving brains or anything? Shambling off in the middle of the night to snack on your neighbors?"

"No!" How could Cassie think such a thing? "She wants to eat and drink, but can't because I don't think her digestive system functions. She talks a lot about when she was alive and used to cook for her family. She's very proud of having won a blue ribbon at the fair for her peach crumble. Family means everything to her. She said that she and the others didn't hesitate to answer my call, that they'd always help defend their family, even from the grave."

"But the others went back. The others went back, but she didn't," Cassie mused.

"No, she didn't." I shook my head, miserable at the thought. "I feel terrible for her. She can't see her family. She can't eat or cook or do all the things she once loved doing. She can't leave my house. It's like she's in some sort of limbo between living and dead."

"Have you tried to send her back again?"

"Twice." I threw up my hands in exasperation. "At first. But she told me this morning that she wants to stay. She wants me to resurrect her. And I think she should have a say in her fate. I can't just forcibly send her back if she doesn't want to go—even if I could figure out how to do it. That's not right. But the resurrection spell I tried this morning didn't work either. I want to give her a choice, but right now I can't promise her either option, and her being stuck in this half-state isn't fair."

Cassie ran her fingers through her hair, tugging the ends. "Crap. *Crap.* I don't know what to do about this. I don't know anything about necromancy."

"I talked to Nash this morning," I told her. "He's going to ask the other reapers if any of them knows a necromancer I can consult with."

She paced, still worrying her hair. "That's a good idea. And I'll ask Lucien. They deal with souls all the time. He might have some clue about how we can return this zombie to the grave."

"No, I want to fully resurrect her," I reminded my sister. "That's what Maude wants."

Cassie stopped and faced me. "It might not be *her* decision, Lonnie. She died. Her soul belongs somewhere. Resurrecting the dead...it's wrong. It'll piss off whoever was in charge of her soul. And I'm not sure I can protect you from the repercussions of that."

Addy had been harboring a soul that had escaped from hell and possessed a squirrel. Lucifer and his minions had gone apeshit over the escape. It had been the biggest ruckus I'd ever seen, all over one escaped soul.

They were probably losing their minds over Maude as well, wondering where she'd gone to and how she'd managed to escape. The demons had come after Addy, trying to force her to give the escapee back. They'd do the same once they realized I had Maude. And they'd probably want me as well, since I'd basically stolen her soul.

"I'll face whatever comes my way for what I've done," I told Cassie. "I'll pay the price. But Maude shouldn't have to. If she wants to live, then I owe it to her to do everything I can to make that happen. This is my fault, not hers."

Cassie grabbed me into a hug. "No, it's *my* fault. I should have searched for a necromancer to tutor you when you were young, or at least some old spell books and manuscripts to help you better understand your powers. What you do…it always scared me, Lonnie. Your magic scares me, so I just ignored it and buried my head in the sand instead of doing what I could to guide you."

I hugged her back. "You're only nine years older than me, Cassie. You were still a kid yourself when Grandma died and Mom took off. Helping me learn my magic wasn't your job, it was Mom's. Don't blame yourself—blame her for leaving. And blame me for not doing more to learn my powers. I'm twenty-four years old. I should have been searching for a mentor, not playing bartender in the human world and animating rats."

Cassie pulled away, quickly swiping a hand under her eyes. "I'll do what I can to honor what you want. And both Lucien and I will make sure you don't get in trouble for this. It was an accident—one that will never happen again."

There was a bit of a question in her last statement. I grimaced, and didn't reply. If my family was ever in danger, I absolutely would do it again—but hopefully I'd know enough next time not to have a soul remain behind, trapped in a decayed body.

# CHAPTER 9

## HADES

*I* headed down to the sixth circle, making my way past all the flames to the third ring. There weren't a lot of heretics by modern definitions, so most of the souls here had been in residence for more than four hundred years. I nodded to a few of the punishment demons I recognized, then stopped at a pit of lava and hot coals with a sofa made of bone in the center of it.

"Hades. Sir." The demon who'd been poking Sarpedon with a pitchfork stood at attention. "Are you here inspecting the modifications?"

The lack of new heretics meant that the sixth circle didn't need expanding, but it was in serious need of a remodel and updates to the punishment areas. I'd been mulling over the changes. Something new. Something creative. The whole lava and pitchforks thing was so overdone.

"No, I need a moment with Sarpedon, if you don't mine."

"Not at all, sir." The demon moved to the side.

The damned soul lifted his head at that, then swung his legs around to sit on the sofa. I waited for him to slip on his sandals, stand, and smooth a hand over his robes before I activated the walkway that would allow him to step from the platform without having to tread on the red-hot rocks.

"Sorry to be disrupting your punishment," I said to the soul. "I have a few questions I'd like to ask you about the necromantic arts."

Sarpedon waved a hand. "It's fine. Different day, same pitchfork. I'm actually glad for a change. It's not the punishment that gets to me, it's the boredom."

"We'll be working on that soon," I promised him. No soul should be bored in hell. The demons might be in the business of eternal punishment, but they weren't monsters.

We made our way around the ring, me nodding to various demons while Sarpedon waved and greeted souls he knew. This was a long shot. I'd already interviewed thirty necromancer souls residing here in hell. Sarpedon was my last hope.

None of them had known anything about the incident. Nor had any of them been able to point me toward any living necromancer who might be responsible. After Sarpedon, my next step would be talking to the crossroads demons to see if any of them had made deals with a necromancer who might have enough power to yank all these souls out of their respective afterlives.

After a few blocks, I spoke up. "When you were living, you were well known as someone who could communicate with the dead," I said. "Can you tell me about that process?"

Sarpedon folded his hands together, his robes swishing as he strolled. "I used incantations and focus items to reach through the veil. The focus item is key. Without it, the soul could be anywhere and it's incredibly time consuming to grope your way blindly through all the different afterlives trying to find the person you seek."

"Do you communicate with the soul where it resides, or

do you remove it from the afterlife and bring it to you?" I asked.

Sarpedon halted, his eyes wide as he stared at me. "Souls cannot be easily removed from the afterlife. That...that requires magic far beyond my knowledge and ability—far beyond almost every necromancer's knowledge and ability."

"But you have this skill," I reminded him. "Many non-European practitioners bring forth souls to animate the dead."

He waved his hands in the air. "I had no knowledge of those people during my lifetime. Academically, it *is* possible to extract a portion of the soul to bring some sentience and self-control to a risen corpse, but not the whole soul. It's not needed. And it's dangerous."

"Dangerous how?" I asked.

Sarpedon blew out a long breath. "Sending a tiny portion of a soul back when you're done isn't a problem. Sending an entire soul back *is* a problem. Sometimes they don't want to go back. It's an entire soul. That risen corpse, that zombie with an entire soul, is not under the necromancer's control. They are under no obligation to do as you say."

It was my turn to stare at him. "So a zombie with an entire soul can't be returned?"

He held up one hand and wiggled it back and forth. "If they don't want to go? There are some spells to kill them again and send their souls back, but those take an enormous toll on the necromancer. Those spells might even kill the necromancer."

"Interesting." We continued walking while I mulled over what Sarpedon had said. Perhaps this other necromancer had been able to return most of the souls, but had died and been unable to return the final one. If so, then I was going to have to deliver some very unwelcome news to heaven's angels.

And everyone would need to be aware that there was potentially a zombie with an entire soul walking around among the humans. Neither of those were ideal situations.

I returned Sarpedon to his punishment, thanking him for his assistance, then made my way clear through the circles of hell to the river Styx. Charon was just docking his ferry, ushering new souls off. The welcoming committee waited, clipboards in hand as they called out the names of the recently departed, grouping them into general categories for transport to the appropriate circle of hell.

I searched through the crowd, spotting who I'd hoped to meet. Bluochol was a reaper. Technically her job was done when she'd untethered a soul from their dead body and handed transport of the spirit over to a nearby psychopomp, but Bluochol was more than a little obsessive about her duties. If she couldn't supervise the transport personally, she came to the arrival zone of whatever afterlife the soul was headed for, and checked the names of her dead off her list. For Bluochol, a soul was never fully reaped until it had crossed the pearly gates. Or infernal gates. Or purgatorial gates.

"There's Eileen Louisa Moalle," she whispered. "And Richard Wilmer O'Connell."

"Two today?" I asked her.

"Four," she muttered, still focused on her list.

A perfect record. This reaper had never lost a soul. She'd never even had a soul show up late. I waited until she'd checked the other two passengers off and stowed the checklist in her voluminous black robes before I spoke again.

"I was wondering if I could have a few moments. I'm working on a special project and wanted to ask you some questions."

She turned to me, her face shadowed by the dark hood. Reapers seldom showed their faces, and when they did, it was revealed to be only a skull underneath their hood. A skull wasn't their true face, but whether it was privacy or a flair for the dramatic, that's all anyone ever got to see.

"Go on, Hades. Are you remodeling the welcome area? If so, I have a few suggestions."

"Not at this time, but I always welcome suggestions." I didn't, but she didn't have to know they'd go right in the trash. "Actually I wanted to ask you about reaping. Hypothetically, if a necromancer were to summon a soul from…oh, say hell. Would you be able to sense it? Could you go forth and reap that soul? Technically, that person should not be among the living."

"Hypothetically?"

I felt the weight of the reaper's stare right through the hood. "Hypothetically."

"If a necromancer were to perform a resurrection, then the person is no longer dead, and there is no soul to reap. We do not reap living souls."

A resurrection. The dead necromancers I'd spoken to had claimed such a thing was next to impossible, a one in a billion chance of success even with the most dedicated, knowledgeable practitioner. But why would the necromancer call forth a over a dozen souls, resurrect only one, then return the others? It didn't make sense. It seemed far more likely that either the necromancer died in the process of returning the souls, leaving one behind, or one soul had stubbornly remained.

"How about a zombie?" I asked. "Not a resurrection, but a soul brought back into a dead body?"

"Well, that is a different matter." The reaper held up a bony finger. "Such a thing would be either a terrible mistake by a newbie, or a deliberate act by a seasoned necromancer who should be punishing souls in the third circle of hell. Zombies usually have only a tiny portion of their soul, easily returned once the undead has served its purpose. Calling forth an entire soul and trapping it in a corpse is truly demonic behavior in the extreme."

I agreed, but I wasn't particularly concerned about the ethics or the morality of the spell caster. It was not my job to judge. It really wasn't my job to go tracking down a lost soul either, but here I was.

"But if that did happen, would you be able to reap the soul and return it to the appropriate afterlife?" I asked.

"The body is dead," she mused. "I do believe I would be able to reap the soul. But it wouldn't show up on my list. The body died quite a while before and the soul had already been reaped once, so such a thing would slip through the system unnoticed. We would not receive the call to reap such a soul."

The good news was if I could find the missing soul, then I could point it out to the reapers and Bluochol or one of her associates could bring it home. But I still needed to find the missing soul, and in a world with over seven billion humans, that would be quite a task.

I thanked the reaper for her time, and ascended to the world of the living, to a place where two roads converged and deals were made. This would be my last stop of the day, then I'd write my reports, grab something to eat, and take another look at those plans for the new Cliffs of Despair.

A man stepped from the shadow of an old oak tree at the spot where the two roads joined. He was handsome by human standards, with golden blond hair and bright blue eyes, but he was not a human.

This was a crossroads demon.

"Greetings, Xavier," I called out.

He grinned and strode forward, hand extended. "Hades! What the devil are you doing here? I thought you'd be nose-deep in the plans for the sixth circle redesign. Or that Cliffs of Despair job. Satan knows we should have modified those eons ago."

"I should be working on both those projects," I told him. "But instead I've been given a side job that has nothing to do with architecture."

Xavier grunted. "That's the way things go in hell. Bureaucracy. Paperwork. A job comes up that no one wants, and they just randomly assign it, as if they drew a name out of a hat."

"Truer words have never been spoken." I waved a hand and two chairs appeared at the corner of the crossroads, in the grassy shade of the oak tree. "Let's sit. I've been on my feet for what feels like a century."

The crossroads demon and I walked to the chairs and made ourselves comfortable. I took a second to admire the beauty of this world. The sun came from behind a cloud, brightening the grass and the pavement. Wind rustled the red and gold leaves of the oak. Fall was truly a beautiful time of year. It was a season of transition, and I loved transition. Birth. Death. Change was a glorious thing.

"This project I've been assigned," I finally spoke up. "It involves necromancy and I find myself at a loss. I've spoken to the dead necromancers in hell and none of them seem to be able to help me. I've spoken to a reaper. Now I find myself needing to locate a living necromancer to hopefully be able to finish this stupid project and get back to my real job."

"I know a necromancer," Xavier announced cheerfully.

I pivoted to face him. "You do?" After all the dead ends I'd hit today, had I finally found a lead?

"Sure. Glenda's sister. Honestly I've never met a necromancer before her. They're kind of rare. Still, she isn't at all what I'd been picturing when I thought necromancer. I'd expected some hook-nosed guy with beady eyes and gnarled hands, sitting by a pile of bones. Babylon is a really pretty woman with red hair and dark eyes. She's a lot of fun, too. Total riot at Sunday night dinners."

"A woman." I frowned, because all the necromancers I'd spoken to so far had been men. Witches were usually women, but on occasion there was a man with witch magic. I guess the same could be true of necromancers, with a woman born with the talent. But male witches usually had minimal powers. A female necromancer with minimal powers wouldn't be able to cast the level of spell that removed all those souls.

"I'm pretty sure she's a woman, but I didn't exactly check," Xavier drawled. "Glenda would frown on that sort of thing even if Babylon wasn't her sister."

This Babylon might not be the necromancer I was searching for, but surely they all knew each other. With such a rare magical art, I would expect necromancers would socialize to share experiences and information. Maybe they all got together once every other year at a small convention. Maybe they had an online chat group.

Either way, I had to meet this necromancer.

"Do you mind introducing me?" I asked, thinking that if Xavier facilitated my meeting her, she might be more open to talking about her magic and other practitioners she knew.

"Sure." Xavier grinned. "How do you feel about bars? And are you free tonight?"

## CHAPTER 10

### BABYLON

*M*aude was streaming Season 3 of Supernatural and working on her blanket when I arrived home. I brought the bone, bits of wood from the sugar maple, and my bag full of magic supplies in and set them up on the dining room table before heading to my room to retrieve the bone that Addy had found. When I returned, Maude was eyeing the setup on my table.

"Are you going to do magic?" she asked, pointing to the bone.

I set the other sliver of bone beside the first. "Yes. A group of elves are under a curse and their spirits are trapped on a mountain in Accident where the werewolves have set up a new compound. I'm going to try to communicate with at least one of the elves to see if I can find out what happened."

"But we eat on this table," she protested, shaking her finger at the bones. "I hate when you do this. I just got finished cleaning everything up from this morning, too."

*I* ate at this table, but I understood what she meant. "I'll clean it thoroughly and smudge afterward, I promise. It's a

78

small house and I really don't have anywhere else to do magic."

She turned a stern gaze my way. "On the floor? In your bedroom?"

A zombie, a woman who was currently a corpse, was scolding me about bones on the dining room table. It was a bit hypocritical, but Maude wasn't to blame for her state, and I would not hurt her feelings by bringing up a sensitive topic.

"The floor isn't always suitable for some magics. Certain things go better if the ritual is at least a foot from the ground. Plus it's uncomfortable sitting cross-legged and scooting around, especially if the spell is a long one."

She raised an eyebrow.

"I have bleach. I have sage," I reassured her.

She sighed. "Okay, but I would never have allowed one of my children to do this on our table. There was that time Jerome brought in a frog from the pond, and I had to practically sand the finish off the table to get it clean again. Tables are for food, eating, and serving implements only. Not crafts. Not frogs. Not magic."

I *really* liked Maude, but this roomie thing was getting old. Helping the werewolves wasn't my only priority. Hopefully Nash would be able to hook me up with another necromancer who could instruct me on how to fully resurrect her. And in the meantime, there were two more spells in those books I'd bought that I wanted to try.

"I've made a decision," Maude announced as I set up the incense. "I want to stay here, but only if I can be in a living body. There's no sense in continuing on like this where I can't see anyone without scaring them, can't eat, can't do so many of the things that make life worth living. I want to have a second life, but I've got a few questions I'm hoping you can answer."

I put down the matches and motioned for Maude to go on. The ritual would need to wait.

"From what I've been seeing on the television, things are different now than they were when I died. I don't know if I can just suddenly be alive again with all the identification and records and other stuff that I'm not going to have. How will I get a job? Or an apartment? Or a car?"

"It won't be easy," I told her. "I can probably find someone who can get your forged identification, but it won't hold up to a lot of scrutiny, so you'd need to be careful what sort of jobs you apply for. You have to be careful not to get arrested or have any reason for someone to look into your background. Jobs that require some sort of security clearance, or volunteer work where you have to go through a background check would be a problem."

Her shoulders slumped. "I'm not sure what sort job I *could* do. I don't understand anything about your computers, or your tiny portable telephones. I was still using an electric typewriter when I died."

"There are jobs you can get while you learn that stuff," I assured her. "Things like cleaning jobs, or working in a kitchen. They don't pay much, but it'll be enough to get you on your feet."

"And afford a place to live?" she asked.

I winced, thinking I'd probably need to put her up for quite a while. "Not at first, but you can stay here until you save up enough to afford a place of your own. Or until you meet someone you'd like to move in with. I know lots of people who rent houses with friends to help split the costs."

Her brows furrowed. "Will I ever be able to see my daughter? Or my granddaughters? Will they ever know who I am?"

"I...I don't know." These were questions I just couldn't answer. "Maybe once you're more familiar with modern life you could meet your family. I know Rita and I can introduce you as a friend. But I'm not sure they can ever know who you really are. People don't believe in magic. They might just think you're crazy and be less likely to want to be your friend."

She sighed, looking down at her hands. "That will be fine, I guess. I'll need to remember that this is a new life for me, not just a continuation of my former one."

I reached out to put a gentle hand on her shoulder. "It *is*. Maybe you could even live in Accident for a while until you felt confident about your new life. With all the supernatural beings there, everyone would understand if you didn't know how to work a cell phone, or had to learn to use a microwave."

"Maybe for a week or two," she mused. "I don't think I'd want to stay there for the rest of my second life. I'm human and I really think I'd be more comfortable around humans. I don't intend to offend you or anyone, and I appreciate the offer. I'd love to meet witches and werewolves and mermaids, but I'm not sure I could live among them full time as just a plain old human whose only special trait is that I've been resurrected."

"Understood, and I'm not offended at all." I met and held Maude's gaze. "I'm going to do everything I can to make this happen for you, but I can't promise anything. Right now I have no idea how to fully resurrect you. I'm working on it, but it may take time."

"Weeks?" Her voice was hopeful. "A month?"

I hated to tell her it might be years. It was so unfair. I felt horrible for doing this to her, then leaving her with no choice but to endure while I got my shit together and figured out how to fix the situation.

"I don't know." I fought back my frustration. "Does that change your answer? If it takes years to figure out how to

resurrect you, but I find out how to return you to the afterlife in a month or two, would you change your mind?"

She thought about that for a moment before responding.
"I don't know. I might. Let me know if you figure out how to
return me to the grave. I honestly don't know how long I'll
be able to wait like this if there's another option available—
even if it's not the option I want."

"I'll definitely let you know," I promised.

"Thank you." Maude eyed the bones on the table once
more. "I'm not sure if I want to be here while you do this. I'm
curious. I've never seen someone work magic aside from the
few times you've done it on me. Is this spell scary? Will there
be blood?"

I remembered the screaming and bleeding as I cut into
the tree trunk to extract the bone. I couldn't guarantee the
same thing wouldn't happen here, even without the tree.

"It might be scary. It's probably a good idea if you stay in
your room with the door closed and the television on."

She nodded, took a step away, then hesitated. "Are they...
the cursed elves, are they in pain?"

Memories of the screaming returned once more. "I think
one is. The others might be as well."

"Then help him first. Help the elf that's in pain before you
help me. I can wait."

She turned around and left. I heard the soft click of her
bedroom door, then the murmur of the television and felt
bad for being annoyed at her earlier. Maude was such a
wonderful person. She'd been a zombie for two weeks. It was
clearly difficult for her to continue like this. And still, she put
another's welfare ahead of her own.

I'd help these elves, but I wasn't going to make Maude
wait any more than she had to. With a sigh, I turned back to
my spell.

It wasn't ideal doing this sort of magic during the day, but as a bartender, my late hours were usually spent working, so I'd learned to make accommodations. I think it helped me in the long run. I might not be conventionally trained. I might have huge gaps in my knowledge. But I could work my magic on the fly, no matter the time of day, no matter the phase of the moon. Few witches could say that, and I was pretty sure that few necromancers could say that as well.

If only I knew any other necromancers to ask.

I might be able to do this at four o'clock in the afternoon, but darkness always helped. I turned off the lights then drew the blackout shades. The heavy curtains and the shades served a secondary purpose as well by ensuring no passing neighbors peeked in the window and saw something alarming occurring at my dining room table. My house was tiny and all of six feet from the sidewalk and the street. People couldn't help but glance in as they walked by.

I lit the candles, murmuring the incantation under my breath. As I'd done in the werewolf compound, I drew runes in chalk around the table, just to make sure if something unexpected happened it didn't go tearing through my house and the neighborhood. As an extra precaution, I lit sage and walked the perimeter of the circle.

When the preparations were done, I arranged the stones in a triangle and placed the bones in the middle. Amazonite for truth. Fluorite for clarity. Apache tears for healing trauma. Smoky quartz for grounding. I sat, folding my hands together and slowing my breathing as I concentrated on the bones.

*Spirits speak, wherever you may be. Tell me your tale. Share with me your sorrows and joys. Give me the knowledge I need to ease you into eternal rest.*

I closed my eyes and reached across the veil.

Darkness. Rot. A foul sweetness. And pain.

It took me a few seconds to realize that I wasn't in any

of the afterlives I'd visited in the past in order to communicate with the departed. I wasn't even across the veil. My
magic had latched onto the focus item of the bones and led
me to where the soul that had once inhabited them now
resided.

A log. A sugar maple tree that had fallen in a storm, lain
across a road, been trimmed and transported to the werewolf
compound, and now sat in Fists's lumberyard. I shouldn't
have been surprised. The spirits were haunting the mountain, and this one in particular was trapped in the log. Of
course my spell brought me there.

*Are you able to show yourself to me?* I asked. *Either in an
image of what you looked like in life, or as smoke or mist?*

I saw nothing but darkness, but the sweet smell of rot was
now laced with the faint aroma of lavender and lemon balm.
Spirits this side of the veil could assume some degree of
visible form but this poor elf was so entrapped by the curse
that he couldn't even manage that.

*Can you speak?*

The smells shifted and changed, as though a wind I could
not feel blew through them. I felt the log shake, and hoped
that none of the werewolves were nearby to witness this.
They were freaked out enough about the haunting without
seeing the log-that-screams-and-bleeds vibrating.

*Help. Me.*

The faint plea broke my heart.

*I'll help you and the others, too. But I need to know what
happened. Who cursed you and why?*

*I stole...was caught...was punished. I didn't mean for her to
punish the others, too. Not their fault.*

I winced, thinking this was an overly harsh punishment
for theft. There had been times in history where a thief
suffered amputation or even death, but this curse was
horrific.

*Is your name Tinsel?* I had assumed so, as the other spirits had repeated his name.

*Yes. It's not their fault. I would have endured my fate, but they should not have been punished.*

*Who cursed you and the others?* Tinsel had said "her," but I wasn't sure if I should be looking for a powerful witch, a sorcerer, or a supernatural being. Many of those living in Accident had the ability to perform specialized magic. Curses would be forbidden under our laws, but clearly someone had done so and gotten away with it—at least until the werewolves had moved to the mountain, and a freak storm had brought this very tree down across their main access road.

*Our Queen.*

I frowned, trying to think of anything I might have learned about the elves when I'd been a child growing up in Accident. But the elves had vanished before I was born, and I wasn't sure the societal structure of the other fae was the same as that of the elves.

*Was your queen with you and the others on Savior Mountain?*

*No. I stole before we left. Almost a century passed, and I thought my theft had gone undetected. But elves live for tens of thousands of years, and the queen must have eventually noticed. She somehow discovered I was to blame. Then she punished us all.*

*She came to Accident and punished you?* I was outraged at the idea that a hostile supernatural being had entered our town and cursed an entire group of our residents, and none of us had known about it.

*Yes. But she could not find the Everbloom and left without it.*

Probably because the bitch was worried that the longer she stayed, the more she risked discovery and the wrath of some truly powerful witches.

*I hid it.* Tinsel's voice was smug. *I knew she would punish me even if I handed it over. And although she implied she would release the curse if I told her where the Everbloom was, it was not a promise or a vow, or even a statement that would be impossible for her to break.*

Fae always kept their word. That sounded like a good thing, but the fairies in town were really good at dancing around any sort of commitment, making you think they'd said one thing when they'd actually said something quite different. It made dealing with them incredibly tricky. If the fae living in Accident were that slippery, then I was sure this queen was...well, the queen of slippery.

*Why did you take the Everbloom?* I asked.

*It blesses the land. Anywhere you plant it, growth flourishes for a mile around. It made our new home feel like...home. We no longer wished to live under the iron rule of the queen, but we loved our homeland and missed it. The Everbloom brought the magic of our land to the mountain we claimed as our own.*

At first I imagined the flower to have some sort of pesticide/fertilizer combination magic, but that didn't seem to be in keeping with the complexity of the fae's reverence for life and the cycle of being. They would be fine with insects, bacteria, and blight, but the Everbloom must allow all life to co-exist without one destroying the other.

I hadn't gone to Savior Mountain at all as a child. Honestly I hadn't gone there until Cassie had given it to Clinton's pack as a way to make peace among the werewolf factions.

*The colors are brighter, the birdsong more melodic. All is in harmony with the Everbloom.*

*Is it still on the mountain?* I asked, because although Savior Mountain was beautiful, it wasn't otherworldly beautiful. And the birdsong sounded like...well, birdsong everywhere else. The werewolves were having the usual struggles with their crops. I'd seen trees that were dead and one good breeze from hitting the ground. I was pretty sure the animals there suffered from the usual ailments. Maybe the queen had found it and taken it with her. Or maybe someone else had.

*It is still exactly where I placed it when I arrived on the mountain.*

I rolled my eyes, thinking Tinsel wasn't any different from the other fae when it came to prevarication and avoiding a straight answer. *Does it no longer work? Life on the mountain seems to be just like life on any other place in Accident.*

*Without elves present, the Everbloom slumbers. It will not release its magic around any but elves. Even other fae cannot stir it to act.*

Then there wouldn't be any damage to the mountain or to the werewolf enclave if it were removed. Tinsel hadn't revealed its location in an attempt to save the others. And it had probably been a good plan. If he'd handed the Everbloom over, they would have had no leverage over the queen.

And I'd have no leverage over the queen—leverage I hoped to use to free Tinsel and the others.

*Where is this Everbloom?* I asked. *Where did you hide it?*

This time I felt a breeze stir the scents of the decaying log around.

*I cannot tell you. If I do, then she will know through the curse.*

*Do the others know where it is?* I pretty much knew the answer, but just wanted confirmation.

*No. But those who know me, who seek with a pure heart and a love for all things living and dead will find it.*

I felt the voice falter, the scent of lavender and lemon balm fading.

*I cannot...she senses...the curse...*

*I release you. Leave and be at peace. Rest. Rest, dear Tinsel, and know that I am always with you. Rest.*

I let go, returning to my body and my house. After a few deep breaths to center myself, I said a cleansing spell, then blew out my candles, put away the spell components and the bones, and wiped off the sigils.

Then I scrubbed down my table and sage-smudged the whole area.

Maude came out and watched as I was working. I half expected her to make some comment about the table needing extra cleaning or something but she remained silent, her arms folded across her chest.

"I listened," she finally said as I finished smudging. "There wasn't any screaming or anything scary. You were just there, but not there. It was like you were an empty body in a chair with candles and incense all around."

"Sometimes I call the spirit to me, but in this case I needed to go where the spirit was," I explained. "He's under a curse, and I realized he wouldn't be able to leave the place where his spirit is entombed."

Maude shuddered. "Were you able to help him?"

"Not yet. I'm working on it, though."

She nodded. "I couldn't just stay in my room. I had to peek out the door, to watch and listen. My family was every-thing to me in my first life. Everything. But this is a new life, and although I still love and care for them, they're not really going to be my family anymore. But you are. You're part of my new family. You brought me back from the grave. You're trying to resurrect me, to help me the same as you're helping those elves. And I feel as if something is linking me to you. I know that as long as I live, I'll regard you as family. Even after my death, I'll still continue to think of you as family."

That was sweet, but a bit disturbing. I liked Maude and didn't mind continuing our friendship—I was the one who'd brought her back from the grave, as she'd said. But I worried that what I'd done had magically linked us. A genuine caring for another was one thing, but a magical binding would be just as horrific as bringing her back into a decayed body.

One more thing to add to my list of sins.

The beep of my phone saved me from answering. I looked down and thought there must be some sort of fate guiding these events, because the text was from Rita.

Rita. The great granddaughter of Maude, Rita.

# CHAPTER 11

## BABYLON

*C*an you swing by today before you head in to work? Rita's text said.

I had a bad feeling about this. Rita was a good friend, but not someone who regularly texted me. I saw her once every few weeks—sometimes only once a month. We hadn't connected since the bonfire other than the usual thank-you-for-inviting-me, I-had-a-great-time sort of thing. Usually one of us would message the other about a lunch get-together, or a band playing at a local winery, but this text felt ominous.

*Sure. Hope all is okay?*

I watched the icon that indicated Rita was typing a response with some dread.

*No emergency. Kristin said you were good with ghosts? Might have a haunting. Might be my imagination.*

I looked over at Maude who'd taken a quick peek at my phone early in the text conversation, but was now studiously examining the newly cleaned table.

"Did you go over to your old house? Visit with Rita, maybe?"

Maude glanced up, guilt written all over her expression. "I was so careful. It was night, and I covered up so no one could see me and be frightened at my appearance."

"How did you get there?" I hadn't even noticed Maude sneaking out. Of course the zombie didn't sleep. Nights must be horribly boring for her with crappy television shows and no one else awake. But how had she made the eight-mile journey from my house to Rita's farm?

Maude looked back at the table, picking at some invisible speck with her fingers. "I tried to hitch a ride with my thumb out, but no one seemed willing to give a woman covered head to toe in a sheet a ride. So I walked."

My mouth fell open. "You walked eight miles?" Actually sixteen miles, unless she'd somehow managed to get a ride back.

"I used to do that a lot when I was alive before," she said, her voice defensive. "It was more like six miles since I cut through fields and backyards."

I shook my head in disbelief, realizing it must have taken her all night just to walk there and back. Not that I could really blame the woman. She'd been trapped in my house for weeks, crocheting, watching television, reading the few books I had scattered around the house.

"I went to the family cemetery a bit to look around. I wanted to visit my children's graves and speak to them. Then I did go up to the house to look through the windows. I thought everyone was asleep. They've updated the kitchen. It looks really nice with the new tile and appliances, and I'm glad to see they left the old fireplace intact. The shelves are gone in the parlor though. I was a little sad about that."

*Lonnie? You still there?*

I'd forgotten to respond to Rita. *I'll be there in thirty*, I told her. I'd be cutting it a bit close getting to work tonight, but I needed to know what Rita had seen.

Probably a zombie in a sheet peeking through the kitchen window.

"I'm sorry, Babylon." Maude tilted her head as she looked back up at me. "I didn't get a chance to really look around when you brought me back and I wanted to see my home. I wanted to visit the graves of my family. And...and I wanted to see the great granddaughter that I'd never been able to meet."

"It's okay." I patted her arm reassuringly. "Next time you want to go visit, let me know. I'll drive you and act as a lookout. And maybe we can get you a black sheet or something to wear so you don't stand out as much."

"I will. Thank you for understanding." She smiled.

I quickly showered and changed into my work clothes, then drove out to Rita's. As I pulled down the long gravel lane leading to the farmhouse, I saw the place in a different light. I'd been here so many times for parties, barbeques, and just to visit, but now I tried to view the farm through Maude's eyes. She'd married her high school sweetheart. He'd driven her down this same lane, to this very same house. She'd sat in the passenger seat, excited to be building a life with her husband, and probably nervous over her new role as a farmer's wife. I envisioned laundry swinging in the breeze on the line that still stretched from the corner of the house to a giant oak. That oak had probably been a lot smaller when Maude had first arrived. The laundry would have been dresses, sheets, overalls, and unmentionables, then in a few years it would have also had tiny baby clothes. She'd sewn, crocheted, cooked, raised a family. She'd helped in the fields when hands had been short and the work urgent. She'd socialized with other farm wives, church folk, the people in town.

She'd won a blue ribbon at the state fair with her peach crumble.

To some people it might seem like a dull life, but I saw it

as a rich and wonderful experience. Home. Family. Maude had built her world around those two things, and she'd been more than satisfied. I only hoped she'd be just as satisfied with round two.

I hoped I could provide her with a round two.

Parking over near Rita's truck, I got out and made my way to the front door. The steps creaked as I climbed, their treads worn with more than a century of traffic. Rita opened the door before I had a chance to knock and ushered me inside, offering me tea or a soda. I declined, following her into the kitchen.

"So…a ghost?" I asked, knowing I couldn't stay long.

She nodded. "A couple of nights ago. I couldn't sleep and saw a white figure in the family graveyard. At first I thought I was imagining things. The bonfire party was crazy fun with the corn maze and everyone dressed up as monsters and demons. I figured it was all still on my mind, or that maybe I was thinking about Halloween and mistook a plastic bag blowing around as a ghost. But it was bigger than a plastic bag. I could tell that when it went by the hay rake."

Maude in a sheet. How the heck was I going to explain this one? "A white garbage bag?" I asked. "It was kinda windy the other night. I could see one of those blowing around and looking like a ghost, especially without much of a moon to see by."

"That's what I ended up deciding it was. I was still wide awake so I went downstairs and got a drink of water from the kitchen then went into the dining room. When I looked back, I saw the white thing by the kitchen window. I tell you, Lonnie, it about scared the pee out of me."

"The plastic garbage bag?" I suggested. I definitely needed to get Maude a black sheet if she intended on continuing this sort of nighttime prowling. The white one was far too visible.

Rita shook her head. "It wasn't. I saw it clearly since it was so close. Lonnie, I swear to you it was someone in a sheet. I was getting ready to call for Ralph to wake up and to go grab the shotgun, thinking there was some intruder getting ready to break into the house, but then it reached out to touch the window, and the person-in-a-sheet didn't have a normal hand. It was like a skeleton hand, except not totally bone. Bone with grayish skin stretched tight over it."

"It was late, a cloudy night with not much moon," I countered. "Are you sure it just wasn't a plastic bag that blew up against the window from the field? Maybe a branch got caught in it, and that's what you saw."

She frowned. "There was a bit of light from the porch because we always leave that on, but I didn't think about it being a branch. Maybe it was a branch. There's a forsythia bush just outside that kitchen window. Maybe the trash bag got snagged on it, and that's what I saw. Although I swear it looked like a person and a bony finger."

"It was late, you were tired, and it was dark," I assured her. "I can't tell you the number of times I've seen something at night that looked like a ghost, or a werewolf, or a vampire."

They *were* ghosts, werewolves, and vampires, but Rita didn't need to know that.

"You're probably right," she admitted. "Still, is there something you can do to check for ghosts or hauntings or something? Sweep the house and maybe the graveyard? It's not just the sheet-person from the other night. Aunt Edna called last week absolutely convinced that my great grandmother had risen from the grave."

I caught my breath. I'd never met Edna, but Maude would have been *her* grandmother. This Edna was probably in her late fifties or early sixties. If she was any younger than that she'd have no real memory of her Aunt Maude.

"Aunt Edna was sixteen when my great grandmother

died, but she definitely remembers her. I'd believe it if she said she'd seen a ghost or something, but this risen-from-the-grave story is freaky and so unlike her."

I tried to calm my heart rate. "Did you ask her why she thought her grandmother was back?"

Rita nodded. "She saw her. She was very fond of my great grandmother. From what I've heard, everyone just adored her—kids, grandkids, dogs, cats. Everybody. She won a blue ribbon at the State fair for her peach crumble."

"She saw her?" I thought for a second. "Maybe your aunt ran across a picture or some belonging she'd inherited and was subconsciously thinking about Maude? Maybe she had a really vivid dream about her."

"Maybe, but Aunt Edna has always claimed to be sensitive to the paranormal. Growing up she was always telling us tales about haunted places she'd visited, and how things had moved on the shelves or how she'd hear footsteps when no one was home. She'd never claimed that someone rose from the grave, though."

"She really believes your great grandmother visited her?" I clearly needed to have a talk with my roomie about her late-night wanderings.

Rita nodded. "She claims to have seen her about four days ago, right before she called me. Aunt Edna said that my great grandmother appeared one night after she'd dozed off watching TV. She was a little disoriented when she woke up, and told the ghost she wished she had that crumble recipe because it had been lost about thirty years ago. She nodded off again, and when she woke and went into the kitchen, there was the recipe written on a notepad by the stove."

"She found it after all these years." Maude was going to be the death of me with these visits. The. Death. Of. Me.

"No, it was a fresh pad of paper with the logo from a new

real estate agent in town, and the ink was fresh. The pen was beside it."

I wracked my brain to come up with some plausible explanation that didn't involve a zombie breaking into one of her granddaughters houses and writing a recipe on a pad of paper. "Maybe she remembered it when she woke up, wrote it down, and forgot she'd done it?"

Rita shrugged. "Maybe. She claims it's Maude's handwriting, just like the original recipe, but that might be nostalgia on her part."

I nodded, happy to accept that as truth. "So, no ghost. Just a trash bag blowing in the wind, and a lost recipe remembered."

"I don't know." Rita frowned. "Aunt Edna claims to have gotten a feeling a few weeks back, like a shivery someone-walking-on-your-grave feeling. She told me it was like all the long-dead family she'd known as a child had suddenly come back. But then suddenly they were gone—all except for my great grandmother. She said she's continued to have this feeling that my great grandmother is here, somewhere close by, watching over us all."

"That sounds like a very comforting feeling for someone to have," I commented, hoping Rita would write this all off as the musings of a woman who claimed to have some paranormal sensitivity and was missing the grandmother who'd died when she was a teenager.

"It *was* very comforting to her." Rita shifted her weight, looking down at her feet. "Would you think I was crazy if I told you I felt the same? I never knew my great grandmother, but I have felt a presence. Not the sheet-person kind of presence. More like something I can't see or hear or even smell. It's a vague impression that someone who loves us very much is nearby—and that this someone would protect us."

"Huh."

I wasn't sure what to say. Lots of spiritual and religious people had those feelings. They might have nothing to do with Maude's presence. But I worried that by summoning her I'd somehow tied the woman to me. If that had happened, it was equally possible that she was tied to the surviving members of her family. She'd had an emotional bond with them, and I'd summoned her and the others to protect not just Addy and me, but them as well. The feeling Rita and her aunt were experiencing could be more than just a general impression of spiritual protection. It could be specifically Maude.

And the sheet thing. I really needed to talk to her about that.

"Was...did your aunt say that Maude was wearing a sheet or something when she thought she woke up and saw her?" I asked.

Rita shook her head. "No. Her eyesight isn't the best without her glasses on, but she said Maude looked just like she'd remembered from her funeral."

Which meant she'd appeared in front of Edna as a zombie in her grave clothes. Great. Wonderful. I was absolutely going to have to have a talk with her when I got back from work tonight.

"Do you think..." Rita's eyes opened wide. "Maybe it was a ghost I saw the other night, and not a trash bag. I'd thought it looked like a person wearing a sheet. Maybe it was my great grandmother, and she'd come to visit me just as she'd visited Aunt Edna. But why hadn't she come inside? I would have welcomed her in. I would have loved to talk with her about her life and the past."

She wouldn't have welcomed Maude-the-zombie in. A wispy figure or someone in a sheet was one thing. A walking corpse was another.

"I'm sure it was just a trash bag," I assured her. "But if

you're concerned, I can come by next week sometime and smudge."

Rita thought about that a few seconds then shook her head. "Thanks, but if it's just a trash bag, then there's no need to smudge or anything. Besides, if it really is my great grand-mother, I don't want her to feel as if she's unwelcome."

As if Maude would be put off by a little sage smoke. Spirits and ghosts would definitely stay away, but a zombie with good intentions could push through the discomfort of the smoky protection and waltz right on in.

"I've got to run," I told Rita, glancing up at the kitchen clock and quickly calculating how fast I'd need to drive to make it to work on time. "Lunch next week?"

"Definitely lunch next week," she told me. "And I promise not to natter on about ghosts and my family the whole time."

I smiled at her. "Honestly? That's a conversation I never tire of. Ghosts are kinda my thing."

# CHAPTER 12

## BABYLON

*I* managed to make it to the bar with seconds to spare, racing through the dining area and clocking in right on the dot. Steve, the daytime bartender, let out a relieved breath when he saw me coming.

"Was getting a little worried here, Perkins," he drawled.

"Think I'd miss Saturday night? This girl's got bills to pay," I teased. Friday and Saturday night were the best for tips, especially if there was a good band playing. Tonight the Bremen Shifters Band was taking the stage, and I hoped to go home with a hefty wad of cash.

True to their name, the group was composed of shifters. They had all been residents of a progressive care facility where the elderly shifters had decided to form a band. They'd gotten their start in Accident, playing at Pistol Pete's bar before branching out to venues in the human world. They were good, and everyone loved that a bunch of old guys were up on stage playing classic rock covers. No one but me and the occasional visitor from Accident knew they were actually a donkey shifter, a canine shifter, a cat shifter, and a rooster shifter.

Steve and I overlapped bartender duties for ten minutes to transition customers and close out his tabs. Finally he clocked out, and with a wave headed out the door, leaving me with six people at the bar, two at a high-top, and drink duties for the rest of the pub. Kirk and Kristen were serving food, and I'd be pouring beer, and making the occasional mixed drink. Although tonight looked like a beer crowd to me.

The band was setting up in the corner and I was filling frosty mugs with amber ale and lager for table eight when two demons walked into the bar.

One I immediately recognized as Xavier, my sister Glenda's boyfriend. It was the other guy who really caught my attention, though.

Tall. Thin, but in that strong-and-lean kind of way. Hair black as a moonless night. Eyes equally dark. Those eyes swept the room as if they were seeing every floor joist and beam, then settled on me.

Heat sizzled through me, and I nearly dropped the mug I'd been filling with beer.

My sisters' boyfriends were all demons, or kinda-demons, and they didn't often party outside of Accident that I was aware of. Hadur, Nash, and Ty were not the extroverted types and rarely even went to the bars inside the boundaries of Accident. Eshu pretty much thought every day was a cause for drunken celebration, but he didn't need to go to a bar to get his freak on. Lucien was either consumed by his duties as the son of Lucifer, or spending evenings with Cassie. Xavier was a crossroads demon and had a hedonistic appreciation for the good things in life, but there were better places to find those than in a little human bar. He certainly wasn't here to make a deal as there were no crossroads for half a mile. Was here to claim a soul? Or had he come specifically to hear the band and brought a friend?

I hoped it was the latter. And I really hoped he sat up at the bar and introduced me to his friend.

I finished pouring the beers and set the tray at the section of the bar reserved for waitstaff pick up. Two women waved me down and I got them another round. As I headed to the other side of the bar, I saw Xavier and his friend sitting on two barstools near the far corner. I ignored a man who really needed to wait a bit before having his fourth beer, and went to greet the demon who was probably soon going to be a brother-in-law.

"Hey Xavier. Who's your friend?" I was going to ask him what he wanted to drink, but the hot guy sitting next to him was staring at me, and honestly I felt drawn to do the same.

"Hades, meet Babylon." Xavier gestured toward me.

He said it as if he'd been talking about me with this man. I hoped it had been good things. Xavier was pretty skilled when it came to communication, so I doubt he would have told his hot friend anything embarrassing. If this was Eshu sitting next to Hades, then the guy would have known all sorts of humiliating things—that sometimes I snored in my sleep, that every time the ragweed bloomed my nose ran nonstop, or that I was wearing a bra I purchased six years ago that was a few threads from snapping because I hated shopping for underclothes. I had no idea how Eshu knew these things about everyone, but he did. And he wasn't shy about telling secrets either.

"You're a necromancer?"

I winced at Hades's incredulous tone, rethinking my opinion of Xavier. Clearly he was just as bad as Eshu. Why for once couldn't I have a chance to make a good impression on a guy I was attracted to before he found out all the gross things about me?

I glared at Xavier before forcing an awkward smile for Hades. "Yes, my magical ability is necromancy."

His gaze swept me again and I knew what he was thinking. Goth girl with red hair that I accented monthly with a box of Fire Engine Red to give it that special color-not-found-in-nature. I looked nothing like my sisters. I *was* nothing like my sisters. And I was so used to seeing surprise and discomfort in people's expressions.

"The only necromancers I have ever met were old, ugly men," Hades commented.

I held my breath, tensing for some sort of backhanded compliment or downright insult that he'd laugh off as "just kidding."

"I didn't expect I'd ever meet a woman necromancer. I especially didn't expect to meet one so beautiful as you."

I felt the red creeping up my cheeks, pretty sure that my face was now the same color as my hair. "Uh...thank you."

I knew I wasn't ugly. Human men found me attractive and interesting. It was the supernatural beings of Accident that tended to regard me with wary caution. That witch-who-animates-the-dead was a label more known than my own name.

"Babylon. That's an interesting name." He smiled at me and my heart about galloped out of my chest.

That had been another sore spot in my life. Everyone assumed I'd been named after the Whore of Babylon, who actually was a goddess of sexuality and not the mythical figure this repressed culture saw as a person to be pitied and despised. My mother had actually named me after the city itself. A place of many languages, where people from all cultures came together to trade and live. She'd had hopes that I'd be another Cassie, a witch who had mastery over many different magical abilities.

Instead I'd animated the neighbor's dead cat before I could even walk.

"Lonnie," I corrected him. "Please call me Lonnie." It was easier, and less fraught with misunderstandings.

"I prefer Babylon."

Once more I tensed.

"I was there, you know. It was a marvel of architectural design, an amazing city of beauty and culture. I wish I could claim such an incredible work of art as my own. One day I aspire to create something as close to perfect as that city."

Suddenly I loved my name and didn't mind at all if he called me Babylon.

"So...what do you do? Do you work for Lucifer in hell? Are you a messenger like Eshu? A reaper?" I asked.

*Hades.* Wasn't he the mythical king of the underworld in the Greek pantheon? As I'd met the men who'd fallen in love with my sisters, I'd learned that reality was often a mix of myths and something a bit different.

"I am the architect." He waved his hand with a false modesty that made me smile. "I've created nothing you'd recognize while among the living, though. I've designed heaven, hell, and purgatory, and often am commissioned for other afterlives as well. Most of my business tends to be in hell as they are experiencing a rapid expansion and are struggling to accommodate the influx of new souls."

Now *this* was fascinating. I leaned my elbows on the bar, cradling my chin in my hands, and prepared to settle in for a good conversation.

"Hey! Bartender! Miss!" Drunk guy whistled, waving his empty beer mug. He was still too drunk for me to serve, but I cast a quick eye along the bar and noted a few people with empty glasses and Kirk standing at the server-station, holding a ticket.

"What can I get you both?" I straightened and held up a finger to tell Kirk I'd be right there.

DEBRA DUNBAR

"Margaritas." Xavier turned to Hades. "She makes the best margaritas."

I did. Giving Hades what I hoped was a flirty smile, I headed down the bar to get Kirk's order and check on my other patrons.

"Miss! Miss!" Drunk guy shouted as I walked by, proving that he was not, in fact, ready for another beer.

"You gotta slow it down, buddy, or you'll end up with an Uber ride home before the first set." I quickly filled a glass of water and set it in front of him. "Thirty minutes and maybe I'll think about getting you another beer."

I practically flew behind the bar, getting Kirk's order, providing three of my patrons with another round, then making the margaritas. I didn't use the bottled, pre-made mix that the bar had on hand. Every day I made a batch of my own with fresh squeezed limes and just a hint of agave nectar. Add tequila, some Cointreau, and a lime wedge, then pour in a glass with a salted rim, and voila! Best. Margarita. Ever.

The band had started up, so I needed to resort to that non-verbal communication that everyone in the service industry knows. I took the margaritas down to Xavier and Hades, gesturing to them that I'd talk later, then dashed off again. The next hour was a blur of drink orders and Rolling Stones covers. When the Bremen Shifter Band announced they'd be back after a short break and the house music came on, I poured another five beers then made my way over to Xavier and Hades.

"Another round?" I'd already served them two each, but demons seemed to metabolize alcohol differently than the humans I served. I wasn't sure if Hades qualified as a demon, but he was clear-eyed, so I assumed when it came to margaritas, I didn't need to worry about cutting him off.

"Absolutely." Hades pushed his empty glass my way. "Are

104

you sure you don't specialize in potions? Because that has to be the most amazing beverage I've ever had."

I felt myself blushing again. That was twice tonight. I didn't think I'd blushed this much in the last three years.

"I'm glad you like it." I hesitated. "You said you know other necromancers?"

He nodded. "Quite a few of them are in hell."

That didn't bode well for my future. "Do you know any who are living?"

"I've been in contact with a few recently." He shot me a quizzical glance. "I assume you already know them. Aren't all of you connected somehow? On a social media group or something?"

I squirmed. "Maybe *they* are but I'm not. I'm a witch and female. And my family has no experience at all with necromantic magic. I do the best I can on my own, but I really think it's time I have a mentor. You know, so I don't inadvertently do something problematic."

He smiled. "A mentor might still get you mixed up in something problematic. Actually, I'm looking for a specific necromancer. I'd wanted to meet you thinking that maybe you'd know who he was, but if you're a solo practitioner and isolated from that community…"

"Oh." I was so disappointed. I'd hoped he was here because Xavier had spoken to him about me and he'd been interested in an intro for romantic reasons. "I guess I can't help you then. Sorry."

I went to turn away and his hand shot out to touch my arm.

"But I'm so glad I met you. It doesn't matter what I came here looking for, I found you. And I'd like to get to know you better, if that's okay."

I appreciated a man who was direct, who didn't hem and

haw about his intentions, so I turned back to him and picked up his empty glass.

"Then maybe after my shift we can grab some early breakfast at the Disco Diner?"

His eyebrows shot up. "Disco Diner? That sounds like a place I want to visit."

I smirked. "Best food in town at three in the morning. Of course, it's the only place open at that time, so in the 'best food' award category, they don't exactly have any competition."

I delivered another round of margaritas to Xavier and Hades. The band started up again and more people came through the door. I was so busy that when the lights flickered and the lead singer announced closing time, it hardly seemed as if an entire night had passed. Everyone finished their drinks and paid their tabs. Xavier slid some cash across the bar then his eyes did a quick back-and-forth between me and Hades.

"You kids stay out of trouble," he teased. "And Hades, *do* remember who Babylon's eldest sister is dating. If you value your contracts in hell, then be a gentleman."

Hades stiffened. "I'm *always* a gentleman."

Darn it. Although given my past relationships, I probably *did* need to take things slow.

I patted Xavier's arm and told him I'd see him for Sunday dinner, then got busy cleaning. Hades watched Kirk, Kristin and me for a few minutes then got up and grabbed a broom. By the time the band had packed up and was loading their equipment in the van, we were doing a final wipe on the tables and running the last of the dishes through the dishwasher.

# CHAPTER 13

## BABYLON

*a*t three o'clock, I was locking the door behind us. I was alert, awake, and energized, my sleep clock adjusted after years of working the late shift at the bar.

I looked around for Hades's vehicle and didn't see any. "I guess I'm driving?"

"I can teleport there if you give me the address. I'm not here often enough to bother getting my own car, and it's easier to just pop in and out of where I want to go."

"Oh." I should have realized that from my sisters' boyfriends, but I never really thought about their transportation methods. Most of the time the couples showed up for Sunday dinner together in cars, or trucks. It never crossed my mind to ponder the fact that those vehicles belonged to my sisters, and that they were usually the ones driving.

"You could steal a car," I said, remembering that Addy's boyfriend, Ty, had done just that when they'd been dating. I was pretty sure auto theft wasn't beyond Eshu, Xavier, or Lucien either. Nash and Hadur didn't seem like the stealing type, and I knew that Hadur had bought a used truck after my sister had released him from the summoning circle he'd been trapped in.

"That seems rather rude." Hades frowned. "What if someone came out in the morning to go to work and found their car gone? What if they had an emergency, and I'd stolen their only means of transportation? Even if I took one from a sales lot, it wouldn't be very nice to deprive a human of a business asset just because I'm too lazy to teleport somewhere."

I doubted any of my sisters' boyfriends would have considered those things. It hit me once more that Hades wasn't *really* a demon, so he'd regard things like theft differently. It sounded as if he regarded humans differently as well. Hades. The architect.

*The* architect. I liked that designation, liked the pride of accomplishment and self-assurance that came with it. He was kind and considerate, but he wasn't shy about admitting his talents. I liked that about him just as much as I liked his looks.

"I'll drive. That way we can talk and get to know each other a bit." I led the way over to my car, trying to squelch the concerns of being in a vehicle with a man I'd just met. Xavier was his friend, and had warned him about being gentlemanly, so I knew I had six hellish demons looking out for me in addition to my witch sisters. But still, I felt uncomfortable. A human guy I'd met one night had pulled something when I was giving him a lift home. I'd been able to handle it with half a dozen undead mice, but Hades wasn't human and I didn't think he'd be as freaked out over zombie rodents as the human had.

My instincts said I could trust him. Xavier had indicated I could trust him. But just in case I animated a squished opossum from the far side of the parking lot, and had him sneak into the backseat as Hades was getting in.

Opossum backup.

"An old friend or a new one?" he asked, seeing the undead animal climb into my car.

"New," I confessed. "Sorry. Necromancers gotta necromance, you know."

I wasn't about to admit that I didn't quite trust him. Although confessing to always having animated corpses around me was probably just as much of a relationship killer as not trusting he'd be on his best behavior.

"I understand." He eyed the opossum once more then climbed into the passenger seat. "Does your new friend have a name."

"No." I'd never thought to name any of my undead. They were just animated. It wasn't like they actually had sentience. They simply were mobile due to my magic and will. Addy named all of her animal friends, but naming a moving corpse felt silly. Like naming a sofa or a fork.

"So, you live in hell?" I broke the silence as we pulled out of the parking lot. "Are there other places you could live? If so, then why hell?"

"I can live anywhere I choose, but I do have some temporary housing in hell. Right now the majority of my work is there, and I wanted to consider my daily commute. Besides, I got a particularly good deal on an apartment in the fifth circle."

I glanced over at him, not sure if he was kidding or not. "I'm sure your apartment is nice, but I don't really understand the appeal of living in hell. Shortened commute aside."

I didn't want to discount the shortened commute. It was a contributing factor for my living outside of Accident, and one of the major reasons my sister Addy had also moved from our hometown. Driving over the mountain each day into the human world was a pain. And for me, I'd felt just as much the oddball inside of Accident as I did outside of the supernatural town. I didn't really fit in there, and I really didn't fit in here either. The difference was that here I could pretend to be human and everyone seemed to accept that. Back home, I'd always be that weird witch who animates the dead.

The roadkill opossum in the backseat chirped, reinforcing just how weird my magic truly was.

"Hell isn't for everyone," Hades confessed. "It's always hot, although it's a dry heat. Some find the cries of the damned to be annoying, but Lucifer specifically wanted the acoustics designed so residents could hear the sound in all corners of hell, so I can't be blamed for that particular feature. Most demons find the background noise melodic, but it's a matter of taste."

"I'm sure it is." I hid an eye roll, thinking that screams and wails were not my idea of pleasant white noise.

"I carefully designed the circles with aesthetics in mind, but hell is basically a purpose-build structure," he explained. "I had certain parameters that I needed to stay within, and expectations to fill. There's only one afterlife that is completely my own design. I'm still working on it, fine tuning the details when I have time between contracts. Sometimes I stay there, but the commute to hell is a bit of a beast. So that's why I have the apartment."

"Me, too. The commute, that is. I've got a little house here in the city instead of staying in Accident," I told him.

He nodded. "I miss it. My own afterlife, that is. Even unfinished, it brings me so much joy. It's wonderful to create something where I don't need to compromise my vision to satisfy a customer's specifications."

In my bartending job I had to make all sorts of drinks that I wouldn't drink if someone held a gun to my head. If it was what the customer wanted, it's what I did. I guessed Hades was under the same constraints.

"You designed heaven and purgatory as well?" I remembered him saying that at the bar. "Were those places closer in alignment to your creative vision?"

He winced. "Not really. Lucifer gives me greater latitude than other customers. The designs for heaven and purgatory had very rigid, detailed specs, so I couldn't be very inventive. The fluffy clouds in heaven had to be an exact density, specific color, size, and shape and distance apart. Harp music only. Choral voices were only allowed to sing three songs on repeat. Pastel pink and blue filters with a certain degree of transparency. The pearly gates at twelve feet on the nose, golden pearl. There was no latitude for creativity at all."

Ugh, heaven sounded just as horrible as hell. I was hearing a theme here and wasn't sure purgatory would be any better. "What do you call it? The afterlife you designed for yourself, that is."

"Hades's Underworld." He shook his head with a laugh. "Not very inventive, I know. My creativity clearly begins and ends in architectural design."

"Hades's Underworld." I smiled. "I'd love to see it sometime. I'll bet it's amazing."

"I'd love for you to visit someday." He sat for a second in contemplation. "Although I had great joy in designing and building it, I want to be able to share The Underworld with others. My work tends to be solitary in nature, but I like being around others. I like hearing voices in the background, seeing demons and spirits as they come and go, taking breaks to have conversation. Living in The Underworld wouldn't be much fun unless others lived there as well."

I shot him a quick glance. "Would that be poaching? From what I've heard, heaven and hell tend to take their soul acquisition seriously. You offering an alternative might bring unwelcome competition."

He sighed. "I'd need to consider that. Perhaps I could

serve a niche audience. Mine would be an afterlife for those who feel out of place in heaven, hell, or even purgatory. There are other niche afterlives available. One more that served a very small group of people shouldn't be significant enough to cost me my contracts with the big guys."

He was so easy to talk to, so interesting and thoughtful. I would love to hear more about his design ideas, his work.

"Should I change the name?" he asked. "Maybe I should call it something like The Meadows?"

I laughed. "That sounds like a suburban housing development—the upper middle-class kind with a super restrictive HOA and neatly manicured lawns."

He smiled over at me, taking away any worry I had that he might be offended at my teasing. "I'm not very good with names. Perhaps you have some suggestions? There are wide-open, grassy spaces, but also wooded areas. There's an eternity of sunsets, fields of flowers, lakes and streams. The homes are magically hidden, only visible when the residents and visitors both want to see them. If a resident wants to be alone, they won't encounter anyone. If they want company, the others will be visible to them."

Interlocking dimensions, constructed so every single resident's wishes were taken into consideration. "It sounds wonderful," I told him. "I'd totally live there. As long as I could continue to work my magic, that is. And for what it's worth, I think The Underworld is a perfect name."

There were so many afterlife options closed to me because I was a necromancer. I doubted I'd meet the criteria for heaven, and even if I did, I doubted if I'd be allowed to have a skeleton army of rats, or zombie birds. That probably wouldn't be allowed in purgatory either. Given my familial connections, I was pretty sure an afterlife in hell would be fairly cushy. I'd probably end up with a nice condo like Hades had, and post-death employment opportunities would probably take advantage of my necromancy skills.

Still… I didn't want to torture souls with zombies and skeletons, even if they deserved it. And it seemed like torturing souls was the only job in hell. I'd have a hard time finding meaningful work or any activities I enjoyed, and I'd probably have to spend most of my afterlife wearing noise-cancelling headphones so I wouldn't need to listen to the screaming twenty-four/seven.

"What about you?" Hades pivoted in his seat to eye the dead opossum in my backseat. "You chose to live away from your family, but you said you don't have a community of necromancers that you work with. Do you have a secondary magical ability in potion making? Is that why your other career is crafting special beverages for others and not in an industry that deals in the spirit world or in the bodies of those who have passed?"

"A necromancer working in the funeral home industry always felt so cliché," I told him. "It may sound weird, but I truly enjoy being among the living. And although I don't make potions, creating tasty and fun beverages, watching people be social and happy, listening to bands play their music and seeing customers dance and enjoy their night, makes me happy."

That wasn't the entire answer. I'd always been the weirdo growing up, and I hadn't wanted to stay in that weirdo-corner by opening up a séance business or working with the dead. Being a bartender made me normal. And I liked being around happy, celebrating humans. There was great purpose in providing closure for grieving families, but it wasn't *my* calling.

Hades's architectural talent was a solitary pursuit, but he loved being around others. I was the same. Bartending gave me that much-needed jolt of human celebration. Necromancy could be such a lonely art, and I found that I needed the living around me.

I turned into the parking lot for the Disco Diner.

"Wow," Hades remarked.

I nodded in agreement. The place had originally been one of those silver-clad, bullet-shaped diners, but new owners three years ago had put a quirky twist on the place. On the roof of the long silver building they'd erected a giant spinning disco ball. Colored lights were trained on it from the side, and the result was a seizure-inducing display of moving colors all over the parking lot.

"Is it the same inside?" he asked.

"Only when someone's having a birthday, or when they play *Stayin' Alive* by the BeeGees," I assured him.

I parked my car and got out, amused to see Hades painted in a wash of moving reflected colors as he climbed out the passenger side. The front door of the diner opened, and as a customer walked out, we heard the faint sounds of Abba's *Dancing Queen*.

"It's not my birthday," Hades informed me. "Just in case you had any ideas."

I chuckled. Good-looking. Kind. Artistic. Interesting. Sense of humor. This guy was downright perfect.

"The food here is actually good, in spite of the quirky theme. They use local grass-fed beef, and cage-free eggs from a nearby farm. It's all farm-to-table."

We headed across the parking lot. When we got to the door, Hades hopped a step ahead and opened it for me. Inside, the disco theme continued in more ways than just the music. Everything was chrome and mirrors. The bench and seat upholstery was shag carpeting. The wait staff wore bell-bottom, white satin pants and shirts bedazzled with rhinestones and colored gems. Both men and women had their hair in the iconic '70s styles that resembled feathered wings.

The hostess had frosted plum eyeshadow in varying shades that curved up to her eyebrows, and lips so glossy they looked as if they'd been lacquered.

Those eyebrows shot up when she saw Hades.

"Usual booth, Lonnie?" she asked.

"Yes. Thanks, Shelly," I replied.

She led us to the back corner booth where I liked to unwind after my shift with a burger and cup of coffee, and watch the patrons. Hades slid into the seat across from me, and picked up the laminated menu.

"I'll admit I was a bit worried." He flipped the menu over, eyeing the selection. "I wasn't around for much of the disco craze and I couldn't remember if there were specific foods or not."

"Like Hamburger Helper and those Snack Pack chocolate puddings?" I laughed at his horrified expression. "Not that I know what either of those tastes like. I wasn't even born during the disco craze. This place has always fascinated me, though. The food is great, and it all reminds me of old pictures of my mom and dad."

Suddenly my good mood evaporated. Pictures were all I had. Faded photos of my parents in their '70s clothing, smiling and looking so much in love. I'd never known Dad. I didn't remember Mom. It was the first time I'd made the connection between this place and them. I'd always loved it here. Maybe that was because I liked disco. Maybe I was trying to connect with a part of my past that had been all too fleeting. I'd need to think more about that, but what I hoped was the first of many nights out with Hades wasn't the right time to be delving into the depressing thoughts of my nonexistent relationship with my parents.

"What do you usually get when you're here?" he asked, pulling me out of the dark hole of memories.

"Burger and fries. Coffee." I eyed the menu. "Their breakfasts are really good, too. French toast with toasted coconut and whipped cream is also a favorite of mine. And the milkshakes are phenomenal."

We ordered, both of us opting for the French toast with coffee. Then we fell into a companionable, easy conversation about food, work, friends, books, and music. By the time we'd finished eating, I was even more convinced I wanted to see this guy again. He walked me out to my car, and I considered inviting him home, but I didn't want to rush this. I'd rushed things with Cameron, falling too far too fast, and that had ended badly. I didn't want whatever this was with Hades to end badly.

And there was one other issue with inviting him home—my roommate. He seemed pretty chill with my magic, but nothing put the kibosh on sexy times like a zombie roommate.

"What are you doing tomorrow night?" I asked instead. "My family does this big Sunday dinner every week. It's at our childhood home and the whole crew gathers together."

Months of dating Cameron and I'd never even thought to invite him to a family function or to introduce him to my sisters, but with Hades, this felt so right. He already knew Xavier. I wanted him to meet my family. I wanted him to see that side of me.

"Cassie isn't the best cook in the world, but she's good at our old favorites," I babbled, suddenly nervous. "And one of my sisters is a professional chef. She always brings something amazing to eat. You'll know people there as well. My sister Cassie is dating Lucien, Bronwyn is dating Hadur, Ophilia is dating Nash—he's a reaper—Sylvie is dating Eshu, Glenda is dating Xavier, and Adrienne is dating Typhon."

His eyes widened. "You have six sisters? Are they all necromancers?"

"No, just me. They're all witches, though. Perkins witches.

I mean, our last name is Perkins. Sometimes my cousin Aaron comes to dinner as well." I twisted my hands together, anxious that he'd say no. Throwing him smack in the middle of family dinner with my rowdy siblings and their boyfriends probably wasn't the best idea for a second date. It would be more like trial by fire. If he could make it through Sunday without running away, then I'd feel free to let my heart ease into his hands.

Second date? Or would tomorrow night be a first date? Did tonight count?

"Goodness, how big *is* your childhood home? That's a lot of people. You must have a twenty-foot dining room table."

He had a teasing little smile as he said it—one that crinkled up the corners of his dark eyes. My heart skipped a beat.

"It's a problem," I confessed. "We added all the leaves into the table, but some people have to eat in the kitchen. Lucien has been talking about knocking out the wall and making it all just one big open space, but Cassie says it'll mean there won't be enough cabinets or countertop space in the kitchen to do any real sort of cooking."

I was nattering away, nervous and worried that he wasn't as interested in me as I was in him. I could tell he'd had a good time tonight, and that he'd enjoyed my company, but that didn't mean he'd want to see me again. Maybe he didn't feel the same chemistry, same attraction toward me that I was feeling toward him. Maybe he thought I was a nice, although weird, girl—but not sexy, not worth actually dating.

He reached out and took my hand. It was an oddly formal gesture, but it still sent butterflies flitting around my chest. He had the long fingers of an artist. I immediately envisioned him wielding a paint brush, executing a complicated riff on a guitar, playing a melody across my skin.

"I'd love to join you and your family for dinner, as long as it's okay with the sister who is hosting. Cassie, you said her name was? I wouldn't want to intrude." Those long fingers rubbed the back of my hand before entwining with mine.

"Oh, it'll be fine." I was all breathless, my voice raspy. I cleared my throat, trying to pull myself together and not come across as a lovestruck teen. "When there's already fourteen people for dinner, one more doesn't cause a problem."

And they'd be thrilled to have me bring a date to meet them. It had been a very long time, and I thought they'd like Hades just as much as I did. Heck, he was a friend of Xavier's. That already made him pretty close to family.

"I've got a lot to get done in the next few days, but I absolutely will make time to see you again." His smile was warm. "And to meet your family. Yes, I'd love to join your for dinner tomorrow night."

"That redesign in hell?" I asked him. "And you said something about changes to the welcoming area? Are the deadlines for those coming up?"

He sighed. "Those are definitely keeping me busy, but this is something else. I don't know how I got saddled with this, but there's a project I've been assigned that has nothing whatsoever to do with architecture or design. The only reason I can think of for Lucifer to put me on this project is because it involves hell, purgatory, and heaven, and most of those people won't even agree to be in the same room with each other. Eshu is the messenger between all three, but I can see why Lucifer might not want him to handle this project solo. It's got the potential to escalate into an outright war if discretion isn't used."

I grimaced, knowing that discretion wasn't a word in Eshu's vocabulary. I adored the guy, and I loved how cute he and Sylvie were together, but he was pretty much chaos on two legs.

"What happened that involves heaven, hell, and purgatory?" I winced. "It's okay if you can't tell me. Lucien is always working on top secret stuff, so I get it."

"I trust you to keep a secret." He laughed. "I know, I just met you, but I trust you. Strange, isn't it?"

My fingers gripped his. "Yes, it is strange. I trust you as well."

He smiled down at me. "This project is actually what brought me to you. I was annoyed and resentful at having it thrust on me, but now I see it as a blessing. Well, it would be a blessing if I managed to avoid a war, that is."

My eyes widened, and I wondered if this was something Lucien was also working on. "It sounds serious."

"It is." He reached out and took my other hand. "A couple of weeks ago a number of souls vanished from hell. They were only gone for a short period of time, then they came back, so it wasn't a crisis. It came to my attention since a few demons were pointing fingers and claiming the missing souls were due to design flaws in hell, but it seems they were summoned by a necromancer."

I froze. "Oh."

"Anyway, the same thing happened at exactly the same time with a few souls in purgatory and in heaven. But one of the souls from heaven did not return. She's missing. They don't know where she is or what happened to cause her to vanish, and they're very upset about it," he went on, clearly not noticing my horrified expression or skyrocketing pulse. "It's a problem because they are blaming hell. They think we stole this soul, and they're going to go to war to get her back. It's not that this soul is particularly vital to them, but the idea that hell somehow managed to swipe her that bothers them." He shook his head. "Of course, hell did no such thing, but heaven is refusing to let the matter rest unless I find the soul and return her to heaven."

"That's...that's terrible." The whole thing was terrible.

Maude wanted to stay, and Hades was tasked with returning her to heaven—which frankly sounded like a horrible place. I needed to figure out how to fully resurrect her and get her a new identity before she was found out. I didn't want a war between heaven and hell, but I didn't want to force Maude into something she didn't want.

And keeping this secret would completely destroy any chance of having a relationship with Hades. Figures. The first guy in months who sparked my interest, and it was over before it began. He'd never forgive my deception in this if he found out, and I couldn't have a trusting long-term relationship with someone with this secret between us.

As much as I wanted to get to know him more, it was probably best if I cut this off right now.

"It sounds like you're really busy. Maybe dinner with my family tomorrow night isn't such a great idea after all," I told him, trying to ease back from the invitation.

"I *want* to have dinner with you and your family." His hands still held mine. "I'll make time for you, Babylon, no matter how hectic things get."

"But the project…" I should pull my hands away, but I just couldn't.

He blew out a breath. "It's a stupid project that I shouldn't even be involved in. Lucifer needs to send his son in to talk to heaven and purgatory. He's the diplomatic type, and is better suited for smoothing things over than me. It's ridiculous. I've spoken with every necromancer I can find, living and dead, and no one knows what happened to that soul. It's heaven's problem, not hell's. And definitely not mine."

His words gave me hope that maybe this could work out between us. If I explained what had happened, told him my dilemma and introduced him to Maude, would he understand? Under normal circumstances I'd assume he would just snatch her up and go, but the Hades I'd gotten to know tonight seemed to be thoughtful, and someone who would understand the ethical difficulties I was facing in this.

But not now. Tomorrow. Or in a day or two, once I had a better handle on the situation with Maude. Then I'd explain to Hades what had happened.

I told him the address for Cassie's house, and let him know what time to be there for dinner. He gave my hands another squeeze then hesitated, bending his head slightly as if he were about to kiss me. I lifted my chin, breath hitching in anticipation.

With a second's pause, he stepped back. Lifting one of my hands to his mouth, he kissed my palm before letting go.

"Until tomorrow night, Babylon." His smile held a boyish uncertainty, and I felt myself smiling in return.

"Until tomorrow night, Hades."

He held my car door open for me as I climbed in, closed it, and waited for me to start my car before vanishing. I sat in the parking lot for a few seconds, grinning like a fool. Then I put my car in gear and drove home.

I liked him. I more than liked him. His old-fashioned manners. His enthusiasm for his job and his creations. His kindness. The way he'd listened with rapt attention when I spoke. The way his fingers had felt in mine.

His tight ass. The dude had a seriously cute butt.

When he'd walked into the bar, I'd seen a hot guy—a guy who physically was exactly my type. But Hades was far more than that. He was wonderful in every way.

He was someone I could easily give my heart to.

But there was only one problem. I'd screwed up, and my vow to make things right with Maude might just cost me the man who could be the love of my life.

# CHAPTER 14

## HADES

Steve was standing at the door of my office when I arrived there in the morning, report in hand. He followed me in and thrust the bound stack of papers into my hand before I even had a chance to make a cup of coffee.

"It's my summary of the interviews with the demons who attacked at the Hoffman farm two weeks ago," he told me.

I had a bad feeling about this report. A very bad feeling.

"Want a coffee, Steve?" I offered in an attempt to delay the evitable.

His eyes nearly popped out of his head. "Uhh, sure?"

"Cream? Sugar?" I asked as the brown liquid spurted into the cup.

"Whatever you decide, sir. I'm honored by your offer of coffee, and wouldn't dare show disrespect by putting any limits on what you give me."

I rolled my eyes then added both cream and sugar before handing it over and turning back to make my own cup. The guy probably hadn't had coffee since he'd arrived in hell. Might as well make it sweet and creamy.

"The demons all say they were not there to attack the

Hoffman family," Steve said as I took my seat. "They claim that they had no intention of hurting any humans in attendance. All they wanted was to retrieve the squirrel."

Again with the squirrels. "What's the big deal about this squirrel?" I asked.

Steve shrugged. "It was Faust."

My eyebrows shot up. Faust had escaped hell and had been on the run for a long time. I didn't pay much attention to gossip, but something I'd overheard tickled in the back of my mind.

"The Faust-squirrel was being given sanctuary by a witch named Adrienne Perkins, who was there at the Hoffman farm. That's why the demons attacked there. It didn't have anything to do with the Hoffmans. It was all about this Perkins witch and the Faust-squirrel." Steve shook his head. "It was a damned mess. Lucien needed to get involved and certain concessions needed to be made. At the end of the day, the demons were told to stand down, and Typhon ended up taking Faust into service as a hellhound."

I grunted. Faust had vanished on Typhon's watch, so it was fitting that he'd be the one overseeing that particular soul's punishment.

Wait. Typhon. Witch. Adrienne Perkins.

Babylon Perkins. A witch necromancer.

The fear I'd been ignoring roared to the surface. Damn it. The Hoffman farm was in the same town that Babylon lived and worked. She and her sister Adrienne had been there at the party when the demons attacked. The Hoffman souls who were buried on the family cemetery had been summoned to defend the farm and their family. By a necromancer. By Babylon.

"There's a genealogy of the Perkins witches here." Steve reached over and flipped the report open. "I'm thinking this Adrienne Perkins witch knows the necromancer. My guess is that he was there at the party with her, and he's the one who summoned the souls. He's the one who has Maude Hoffman. You'll have to be careful because the Perkins witches are powerful and connected to some high-level folks here in hell, but I'll bet the necromancer is a friend of hers."

No, *she* was Adrienne's sister.

Babylon had Maude Hoffman's soul. I couldn't admit this to Steve or anyone else. I could barely admit it to myself. The angels had given us a four-day deadline and we were already one day into that, but I needed to try to stall as long as I could. In the few short hours I'd spoken with her, I felt as if I knew Babylon Perkins. She'd called forth over a dozen souls from their afterlives, and from the situation Steve had outlined, she'd had a good reason to do so. I was sure she had an equally good reason for keeping Maude Hoffman's soul.

I couldn't just type up my report and turn it in. I couldn't reveal to anyone that she was the necromancer responsible for this mess. I couldn't do that to her.

One evening chatting over French toast and I was already falling in love with the beautiful necromancer. But even if I didn't have feelings for her, I wouldn't turn her in. Babylon was a good person. I didn't want to see her in trouble for this. I wanted to help her any way that I could.

So I'd bury this report of Steve's. I'd send him off on some wild goose chase, tracking down someone else—anyone instead of Babylon. It would buy me time—the time I needed to hopefully find a way out of this mess.

# CHAPTER 15

## BABYLON

"*Y*ou had a date?" Maude's eyes sparkled with excitement. She sat at the kitchen table and motioned for me to do the same.

"I *think* I'd call it a date." I grabbed my cup of coffee and plopped down in the chair across from her. Getting home at almost five in the morning had been my excuse for not telling Maude about my evening. I'd gone straight to bed, snagged five hours of sleep, and was up at what for me was an early hour. I had things to do, first among them telling my roomie about last night.

"Tell me all about him." Maude sighed. "I wish I could meet him, but I know you can't exactly introduce a young man to me when I look like I just crawled out of the grave."

I winced. "It's not that. He's looking for you, Maude. When I summoned you and your family, heaven, hell, and purgatory noticed. The others went back, so no one prioritized checking into what happened, but you didn't return."

She frowned. "They sent him to track me down, and he traced me to you. Oh, Babylon! I'm so sorry. My being here is going to get you in trouble, isn't it?"

I sipped my coffee and rubbed the sleep from my eyes, trying to think of a way to tell her the details without making her feel guilty about her desire to live a second life.

"If what I've done gets me in trouble, then that's on me. It's not your fault I summoned you. I'm the one who screwed up."

Maude didn't appear convinced. "So what happened? I'm guessing he didn't figure it all out yet, or I wouldn't be sitting here and you wouldn't be calling last night a sort-of date."

"He knows I'm a necromancer but doesn't suspect I'm the one responsible for yanking you out of heaven," I explained. "Xavier, a crossroads demon who is dating one of my sisters, introduced him to me. I get the impression he was going around and talking to necromancers about the incident, trying to investigate, and thought I might know who was responsible."

I told her the whole story, from the moment Hades came through the door to him kissing my hand in the parking lot of the Disco Diner.

"He sounds wonderful." Maude reached out and patted my arm. "You should tell him about me. People should never begin a relationship with such secrets between them."

"I will tell him. Just not yet." I eyed my coffee cup, miserable that I might not be able to help Maude. "I want to see if there's any hope of fully resurrecting you first, because me telling him is going to end up with you dead once more."

She leaned back in her chair, studying me for a moment. "Then so be it. I would love to live a second life, but not if it ruins this chance for you and a nice young man. I had one good life. And you said I came from heaven, so being dead again wouldn't be so bad. It's not like I'd be going back to torture and lava pits."

"It's clouds and harps and choirs singing the same three

songs over and over on repeat," I insisted, because that sounded just as bad as torture and lava pits in my book.

She shrugged. "Even if you resurrect me, I'll end up back there in another fifty years or so. Like I said, I don't want my desire for a second life to ruin yours."

I slid my arm back, catching her hand in mine. Gently. Because I didn't want to accidently damage the fragile, decayed skin covering her bones.

"You listen to me, Maude Hoffman." My eyes met and held hers. "You living a second life is not going to ruin mine. I will do everything within my power to help you have a second life here, fully resurrected and able to walk around, work, bake, make friends, maybe even find love. If Hades can't understand the reasons why I want that, then he's not the man for me."

Oddly, the more I thought about confessing, the better I felt about it. Hades struck me as a thoughtful, logical man. He'd understand that I'd screwed up, that I was trying to make the best of it. And if he was who I thought he was, he'd help me *and* work to prevent a war between heaven and hell.

"Hades got roped into this thing. He's not a demon, and it's not at all in his job description to track down lost souls," I told Maude. "He's an architect. He's smart, creative, and kind." I suddenly had an idea. "If I manage to resurrect you, and you live out a normal human lifespan, then after your death, maybe you could go to Hades's afterlife. It sounds lovely. I'm hoping to go there after I die."

I told her about Hades's Underworld and described the afterlife he'd created.

Maude smiled. "That sounds lovely. Much better than the clouds and harp music, although I don't think I'd really mind clouds and harp music."

I let out a breath, so happy that I'd told Maude. I felt better about the whole situation. And I was resolved to tell

Hades the whole secret after dinner. Or maybe the next day. Soon. I'd tell him soon.

And now for the less pleasant part of our conversation.

"When I went to see Rita yesterday, she told me that her Aunt Edna is convinced that you have risen from the grave." I frowned at Maude. "This Aunt Edna thinks you were standing in front of her—not in a sheet this time—and that you left her the recipe for the peach crumble."

Instead of appearing defensive, Maude seemed to deflate before my eyes.

"I'm so sorry, Babylon. I won't do it again. She was asleep, and I thought she'd assume she dreamed I was there."

"And dream the recipe you left for her?" I asked.

Maude looked down at the table. "She told me she'd lost it. That was my award-winning peach crumble recipe. I couldn't let it be lost forever. Future generations should be able to make and enjoy my famous peach crumble."

I sighed. What was done, was done. And Maude had promised not to do it again. "I hope I can find a resurrection spell that works. Then you truly can visit your family. Maybe you can say you're a long-lost distant cousin or something."

She smiled. "I'd like that. Instead of Maude Hoffman, or even Mary Ann Hoffman, I think I'd like to be known as Ann Flemming. That was my maiden name, you know. And I always liked my middle name. Ann Flemming. What do you think?"

"I love it. Should I start calling you Ann?" I asked.

She thought about that a moment. "After I'm resurrected. It will be my new name. And if you can't resurrect me, and I need to return to heaven, I'll continue to be Maude."

Now I was doubly motivated to make sure Maude had a second life—one as Ann.

\* \* \*

I WAS UP EARLY NOT JUST to talk to Maude, but to go to Accident and see what I could find out about elves—one elf in particular. But before I went to speak to the fairies, I needed to talk to Cassie.

I showered and took special care picking out my clothing. Then I added another cute outfit and some dressy boots to a duffle bag, just in case I got dirty in the course of my investigation.

After all, I had a man to impress at tonight's family dinner.

It took quite a lot of banging on Cassie's door for her to answer. I saw both her and Lucien's cars in the driveway, so I wasn't sure what was taking so long until she opened the door. My sister's hair was a tangled mess, her lips swollen, the T-shirt she wore was on inside-out and backwards. As she swung the door wide, the hem of said shirt rose and I quickly averted my eyes.

"You're flashing some snatch there, Cassie. Couchie alert," I told her.

Yes, she was my sister, but there were some things I really didn't need to see—especially at ten o'clock in the morning.

She ignored me and ran a hand through her hair, lifting the shirt even higher.I forced my gaze to remain on her face.

"This couldn't wait until tonight?" she asked with a sigh.

"Honey? I've got the whipped cream and cherries ready!" Lucien's voice called from upstairs.

I so didn't want to know.

"No. It can't." I pulled her outside, hoping none of the neighbors were looking our way. "Xavier came into my bar last night with a guy named Hades. He's from hell. He's their architect, but he's looking for a necromancer because of an incident a few weeks ago."

I told her the whole story. She raised her hands to rub her

face and in the process flashed the entire neighborhood full-frontal.

"Crap. Why couldn't the woman's soul have been from hell? Lucien could have covered that whole mess up and given you time to figure out how to make it right. But heaven? Those angels are assholes. Of course, they're blaming Lucifer. Of course, they're threatening war."

"I told Maude and she's resigned to the fact that she made need to go back to heaven," I explained. "But I'm still going to try to do everything I can to help. If you have any ideas, I could really use them right now."

She started pacing back and forth across the porch. "I'm going to tell Lucien. Maybe he can stall, or even smooth things over with heaven. He's not quite as on-the-outs with his grandfather as the rest of them, but I don't want to put him in a bad position over this. Maude may just need to go back to heaven, Lonnie."

"I know." The only good in this whole thing was that the demons and angels should at least know *how* to get Maude back to heaven, where I clearly didn't. If I couldn't figure out a way to resurrect her, then at least she wouldn't be trapped here forever as a rotting corpse.

"You said you spoke with Nash?" She waited for my nod. "I'll see if Lucien can refer us to any living necromancers. If not, I'll send him to hell to talk to the dead ones. *Someone* has got to know how to resurrect this soul."

Relief swept through me. Cassie wasn't giving up. She'd help me try to give Maude a new life. She'd enlist the help of the son of Satan. She'd stand in front of me and protect me from any fallout my actions may bring down upon my head.

She was my sister, but in so many ways she was more of a mother than the woman who'd given me birth.

"Thank you." I blinked away a sudden spurt of tears.

"Oh, stop." She grabbed me into a hug and I didn't care that she was only wearing a threadbare T-shirt.

I sniffed when I finally pulled away, swiping a finger along the bottom of my eyes. "There's one more thing. The guy that Xavier brought into the bar? The one who is looking for Maude? I...I went out to breakfast with him after my shift. And invited him to dinner tonight."

Her eyes widened. "Was this before or after you knew he was trying to hunt you down?"

I grimaced. "Before. But I trust him. I'm going to tell him what I did, tell him about Maude. But after dinner. Or maybe tomorrow sometime. I like him, Cassie. I really like him. And I don't meet a lot of guys I feel this way about."

Her eyes met mine, holding my gaze for a while before she let out a long breath. "I want you to be happy, Lonnie. You've lived so much of your life without the things the rest of us had. Parental love and affection, and guidance. Heck, even our grandmother died when you were so young."

"I had you. I had six sisters who loved me and were always there when I needed them." I gave her a watery smile. "That's more than a lot of people have."

"We were children, too." Her voice was soft and full of sorrow. "I was thirteen—far too young to be a mother to anyone. I did my best, but I'm still very much aware of what you lacked growing up."

It was me this time who reached out for her. "I lacked nothing. I didn't need Mom or Dad, or even Grandma when I had the six of you. And Cassie? You were an amazing mother figure, even at thirteen. I never doubted you loved me, that you'd do everything to protect me. Hell, you stepped up and convinced a judge to not only emancipate you, but to award you custody of six younger siblings. That alone should prove how capable and strong you are."

131

She laughed, hugging me tight. "Well, magic had a little bit to do with that judge's ruling."

"Even more proof of how capable and strong you are," I teased as I pulled away.

She chucked. "So, one more for dinner. You do know that not only are your sisters going to rag on your for this, but every one of our boyfriends is going to drag this guy out into the backyard for a stern talk about what it means to date a Perkins witch, and how they'll kick his ass if he hurts you."

"I wouldn't expect any less." I eyed my watch. "So you'll tell Lucien? I'm going to work on the issue at Savior Mountain today, but this thing with Maude is of equal importance."

She nodded. "I'll tell him. And I'm here for you—either about the cursed ghosts on Savior Mountain, or you trying to resurrect your zombie, or for relationship advice with this new man."

I grinned, thinking that Cassie was probably the last woman I wanted to take relationship advice from. She and Lucien were amazing together, but my eldest sister didn't have the best track record with men before him. Besides, Cassie was always the dominant one when it came to men—in or out of the bedroom—and liked her relationships to be rough-and-tumble. I tended to prefer the nerdy guys, and liked a kinder, gentler, snuggly type of man. What worked for Cassie would probably never work for me.

"Sounds good," I told her. I might not take her advice, but I was always open to hearing it. It was the least I could do for the woman who'd raised me.

"Cassie?" a voice shouted from upstairs. "Whipped cream is melting. And I'm getting a cramp in my left hip from the ropes."

I so didn't want to know about this.

"Thanks," I told Cassie, backing away as quickly as I could. "I'll see you tonight. For dinner."

"We're having pork ribs." She spun around, flashing me a view of her ass. "Coming, sweetie. And I'm bringing the crop."

I cringed, practically running for my car. Hopefully there would be no whipped cream or cherries tonight with the pork ribs, because I now had a visual that I simply couldn't get out of my head.

# CHAPTER 16

## BABYLON

*D*riving the short distance from Cassie's house to the jewelry store on Main Street, I thought about what my sister had said. It would all work out with Maude, I knew it. Lucien would handle the diplomatic issue between heaven and hell. He and Cassie, with the help of my other sisters and their boyfriends, would get me in touch with any necromancer living or dead who could help me with the resurrection. I'd talk to Hades, and he'd understand. It was all going to be fine, I knew it.

So now I could focus on the cursed dead haunting Savior Mountain.

The door chimed as I walked into the jewelry shop. Mirabelle was visible through an open door to a back room, typing on a laptop. Another fairy named Amilae cleaned the glass display counters in the front part of the store. A gorgeous set of onyx earrings caught my eye, but I forced my gaze away. I was here for information not to buy something, but even with my natural resistance, the fairy magic pulled at me, making me yearn for the jewelry.

"They'll look beautiful against your bright red hair,"

Amilae said, pulling the display tray from the glass cabinet and placing the onyx earrings on the counter.

"They would, but I'm not here to shop today." I smiled and forced myself not to look at the earrings. "I was hoping you or Mirabelle could answer some questions about the elves that used to live on Savior Mountain."

The fae magic ended with an abruptness that took my breath away. Mirabelle poked her head around the corner of doorway to the back room, then walked out into the shop toward me.

Amilae pouted, sliding the earrings back into the case. Both she and Mirabelle had silvery-gray skin and unnaturally large emerald eyes, but Amilae's hair was a short cap of lavender, while Mirabella had elected for a cascade of raven curls. Accident was a place where the supernatural could relax and be themselves without needing to hide their true appearance, but the fae were one of the few groups who continued to use their glamour here. I'd always assumed it was more of an aesthetic for them, changing their appearance like others changed their clothing, but over the years I'd begun to wonder if they did it because they didn't trust anyone with even a glimpse of their true forms.

"You wanted information on the elves who used to live on Savior Mountain?" Mirabelle asked. Her luminous eyes met mine. "There is a price for knowledge, you know. There is a price for everything."

I held back an exasperated sigh. Everything involved a bargain with the fae. Normally this wasn't a problem for any of my sisters. Addy would have offered to pied-piper some mice from their back room. Bronwyn would have offered to magically enchant an item of jewelry. Sylvie would have crafted a charm for them, and Ophelia would have divined what stones customers would want most next month. Glenda would have baked them a cake. Cassie would have thrown her weight around as the head-witch of Accident, and come up with some compromise involving her attendance at a festival or protective runes around the store. My magic wasn't really suited for this sort of exchange, though. I got the feeling these two fairies wouldn't want zombie birds, or butterflies.

A séance? But did the fae even have any dead to communicate with? They seemed immortal, although I supposed they could be killed. The elves certainly had been killed, and the fairy were related somehow to elves, brownies, and the other fae races.

"Do you have a ghost problem?" I asked, trying to figure out something I could offer in exchange for the information. "An undead problem? Or would you *like* to have an undead problem? I can make that happen for you."

"She could send a bunch of skeleton cats over to harass the gnomes," Amilae suggested. "Undead cats chasing them around for a day or two might motivate them to pay for that necklace they still owe on."

Mirabelle shook her head. "I'm not going to start a war with the gnomes over a few hundred dollars. Besides, I like that they owe us. Gives me leverage."

"She could buy the onyx earrings." Amilae gestured at the display case. "Full price. No haggling."

Mirabelle glared at her. "She gets the earrings in that bargain, not earrings *and* information. Amilae, you seriously need to work on your negotiation skills. The customer does not come out ahead in a bargain. *We* come out ahead. Or, if they're very smart, it's an even exchange."

Amilae frowned. "But last week when Marcus was in here, you said—"

Mirabelle cut the other fairy off with a wave of her hand. "*I* came out ahead in that bargain. I just whined and complained and made Marcus *think* he got the best of me.

That's how this works. Goodness, girl. You have a lot to learn before I can turn you loose on customers."

"Your firstborn child,"Amilae blurted out. "We'll give you the information in exchange for your firstborn child."

My mouth dropped open, but thankfully I didn't need to reply.

Mirabelle swatted the other fairy. "Don't be ridiculous. She's a *witch*. She's a *Perkins* witch. And she's a necromancer. Her firstborn child would probably kill us all and animate our corpses. That's no bargain."

"I'll buy the earrings at full retail, and I'll make sure no undead disrupt your Hallow's Eve celebrations this year."

Amilae frowned. "We've never had a problem with undead disrupting our celebrations. Why would we need protection this year?"

I stared at her for a second. "Because I can guarantee that without my assistance, a dozen dead deer in an advanced state of decomposition will disrupt your festival."

Amilae's eyes widened. "You can divine the future? Like Ophelia?"

Mirabelle swatted her again. "No, you fool. She's saying... oh, never mind. Go in the back and grade the emeralds. I'll finish up with Babylon."

Amilae went into the back room, grumbling under her breath. We watched her go, then Mirabelle pulled the onyx earrings out from under the case.

"We have a deal, Babylon Perkins. You buy the onyx earrings at full retail, and ensure our festival is undisturbed by undead, and I will tell you all I know about the elves on Savior Mountain."

I bit back a grin. Cassie wasn't the only Perkins witch that could play hardball when she needed to. I handed her my credit card, slipping the little silk bag with the earrings into my purse when we'd completed the transaction. Then

Mirabelle leaned on the counter, ready to deliver on her part of the bargain.

"The elves arrived in Accident one hundred years ago. I went to welcome them, and see if we could work something out between us. My sisters and I were eyeing one of the springs up on Savior Mountain for a festival. They had just arrived from their homeland and were unfamiliar with life here—among other supernaturals as well as in Accident. Aside from a brief meeting with Isadora Perkins, the head witch at the time, they didn't speak to anyone, or socialize with anyone. When I went up there, they seemed to be on edge and frightened." Mirabelle shrugged. "Elves are weird. It's not like the fairies were going to want to be their besties, so I gave up on us using the spring, and left."

"How many were there?" I asked.

"Twelve or thirteen." She frowned. "Thirteen. Yes, there were thirteen."

"How long were they here before they vanished?"

She shrugged. "Seventy years? None of us really know. After a decade or so, we all kind of forgot they were up on the mountain. They never came to town, never interacted with anyone else in Accident. They could have been gone for a decade and we wouldn't have noticed."

"But someone eventually noticed," I commented.

Mirabelle nodded. "I don't know who, though. Someone must have gone up there and found their village abandoned, because the gossip spread like wildfire. No one knew exactly when they'd left or why. They were just all gone."

"Everyone thought they'd gone home," I said, remembering what I'd been told as a child.

"Yes. There was no sign of violence, no bodies, no burned or destroyed buildings. Not that anyone would have reason to attack them. They kept to themselves, and we pretty much forgot all about them."

"What do you know about their homeland?" I asked, knowing who had cursed the elves and why, but wanting to get as much background as I could on the situation.

"Fae lands are worlds of illusion and magic." She smiled fondly. "We all can come and go as we please, through the mists or mirrors, or a beam of moonlight, or the rings of mushrooms or stones on hallowed ground. Such beauty. Such elegance. We all love and cherish our homelands."

"Then why stay here?" I wondered. Mirabelle had been living in Accident for over two hundred years—which probably wasn't all that long in the life of a fae, but seemed an odd length of time for someone who loved their homeland so.

"It's interesting here. We seek that which is new and unique and beautiful. The world here is raw and harsh, but that has its own appeal. Some fairies come and go—like a day-long vacation that lasts a few years or a decade or so. Others enjoy the experience and remain for hundreds of years." She sniffed. "Clearly these elves found themselves unable to adjust."

"They were cursed," I told her. "They were murdered and cursed, and their spirits now roam Savior Mountain, crying out for justice."

All the color drained from Mirabelle's silvery skin. "Wwwwhat?" she stuttered. "Who? Who would do such a thing? Did they break the rules? Was it Isadora Perkins who cursed them?"

At first I was shocked that Mirabelle would think that one of the Perkins witches would be responsible, but we were the law here in Accident. It was inconceivable to think that someone could have snuck into Accident on our watch and cursed an entire group of elves, so she'd immediately jumped to the conclusion that this was a punishment meted out by the ruling witch at the time.

"No, it wasn't Isadora who cursed them, it was their elven

queen." I watched for her reaction, but the fairy only frowned. "From what I've been told by the dead, an elf named Tinsel stole an artifact called the Everbloom from his queen. He thought the theft had gone undetected. He and the others came here and hid the Everbloom on Savior Mountain. The queen found out and came for them."

Mirabelle sucked in a breath. "Well, then justice was served. Death is the punishment for theft. But did their queen go to the head witch when she arrived, present her grievance and evidence, and get the witch's approval for the punishment?"

I needed to check the journals in the attic, but I was pretty sure the answer to that would be no. If the queen had gone to the head Perkins witch at the time, then the elves would not be haunting Savior Mountain. If there had been evidence of theft, the head witch probably would have revoked permission for the elves to remain here, and allowed the queen to take them back to their homeland for punishment, but she wouldn't have approved the curse.

"I doubt whoever was the head witch knew anything about it." I hated to admit that flaw in our protection of the residents of Accident, but I couldn't completely blame my great grandmother, or my grandmother. Some Perkins witches were stronger in magic than others. The weak ones did their best, but sometimes their best wasn't enough. We were lucky. There were seven of us, and Cassie was one of the strongest witches the town had seen in generations. Not all the previous witches had been so lucky.

"Savior Mountain." Mirabelle grimaced. "They're cursed and haunting Savior Mountain, where the new werewolf clan has taken up residence. And we all know how werewolves feel about ghosts."

"Yeah." I ran a hand through my hair. "Any ideas on what

sort of curse the elven queen might use? And how to break it?"

She shook her head. "Your sister Sylvie might have a chance at breaking the curse, but I doubt it. Fae queens are strong in their magic. This queen is most likely the only one who will be able to break the curse and she'll have no reason to want to do that. Unless you have something she wants, that is."

Fae and their bargains.

"The dead have told me she was seeking the Everbloom and that they didn't reveal its location to her," I said.

Mirabelle winced. "I'm sure their deaths and their cursed afterlives are agonizingly painful. They stole from their queen and refused to return the object. I can't say I blame her for cursing them all."

"The dead elves believe she would have done the same if they turned over the Everbloom, and that holding it back gave them the only leverage they have."

"Some leverage." The fairy rolled her eyes. "Dead, cursed elves can't exactly bargain. Although, if she wasn't willing to give them lenience if they returned the stolen item, then I guess they had no reason to tell her where it was hidden."

"It's been roughly thirty years since they were cursed," I pointed out. "What are the chances that the queen might be willing to bargain now? If we find the Everbloom and offer to give it back if she reverses the curse, do you think she will?"

Mirabelle pursed her lips. "It'll depend on how valuable the item is, and how pissed off she is at the elves who stole it. The desire for vengeance is often far more important than any artifact, and her cursing them definitely sent a message to anyone who was considering doing the same. If she reverses the curse, she might appear weak."

I let out a breath, feeling absolutely frustrated. I couldn't help Maude. I probably couldn't help the elves either. Or Clinton's pack. There had to be *something* I could do.

"Everbloom." Mirabelle tapped a long ice-blue nail on the glass counter. "Enchanted flowers are highly prized. Perhaps the queen's anger has dampened down a bit, and she's missing her possession. She might be willing to trade. And you're in a position to offer something in addition to the stolen item to sweeten the deal."

"Me?" I eyed her in astonishment, wondering what a necromancer could give an elven queen.

"Well, not you specifically. Your sister Bronwyn creates some beautiful enchanted items, many of them fit for fae royalty. If you offer the Everbloom *and* one of Bronwyn's lovely sculptures, their queen might consider the bargain."

I knew Bronwyn would agree to help, but that wasn't my only obstacle. I needed to find the Everbloom, then figure out how to go through the mists into the elven lands, find the queen, make my offer, and hope she was in a bargaining mood. It would be easier if Sylvie could break the curse, and I fully intended to try that option first. But I needed a plan B.

And I needed to do something fast, before Clinton's pack dissolved, ran back to Dallas, and we were back where we started with the werewolves.

## CHAPTER 17

### BABYLON

"*T*his isn't going to be easy." Sylvie and I stared down at the bleeding log that Fists had hidden in the rear of his wood lot. "I haven't even lit a candle and I can feel the magic pouring off that thing."

"But do you think you can break the curse?" I asked.

I'd gone from Mirabelle's jewelry shop straight to my sister's house, then drove her up Savior Mountain to the werewolf compound. Clinton and a handful of the others were a respectful hundred feet away. I was ready to have them move farther back depending on what Sylvie was planning. Breaking spells always resulted in a magical backlash. Usually that backlash could be contained or redirected, but sometimes things went boom and I didn't want Clinton or his people to be hurt.

"Nope. Not the slightest chance, but if being with Eshu has taught me anything, sometimes the longshot happens when you least expect it."

I glanced around nervously. "With Eshu, that longshot usually comes with chaos and destruction."

Sylvie chuckled. "True. Which is one of the reasons I didn't bring him today."

A demon partner amplified a witch's abilities, and witches also enhanced a demon's power in return. But Eshu wasn't truly a demon, and his effects on Sylvie's powers often produced unexpected and disastrous outcomes.

Sylvie lit a dark red candle and changed as she waved it over the log. After a few minutes, she blew out the flame and set the candle down.

"The spell is woven into the wood." She frowned. "Tightly woven. And it binds the dead elf's soul and body both. Hurting the wood causes the elf great pain."

"So we can't cut the body out of the tree?" That had been one of our options. Sylvie had thought if the spell had been mainly confined to the tree, removing the remains would break the magic.

"No. If we managed it, the spell would continue to bind them together. I doubt even transporting the bones outside of Accident would break the spell."

"Can you unravel it?" I asked. That had been a second option. Sylvie said that curses were like knitting. If you snipped a thread and pulled, sometimes the whole thing came apart."

"That's what I'm going to attempt." She glanced over at the werewolves. "You guys might want to move about twenty yards more away."

"My *house* isn't twenty yards more away," one of them pointed out in a panicked voice.

Sylvie waved a hand. "This won't hurt your house. It probably won't hurt you either, but it's best to take precautions."

The werewolves moved back—they moved far back. I could barely see them hiding behind the trees at the edge of the compound. Sylvie glanced around to make sure the area was clear, then she pulled a velvet bag out of her pocket. Opening the bag, she carefully removed several shards of glass.

I leaned closer and realized they weren't glass, they were pieces of a broken mirror.

"*Shatter.*" With that one word, Sylvie plunged the piece of mirror into the tree. Her magic pressed against me, nearly forcing me to the ground. I gasped, amazed at how her power had grown over the last year. I didn't often witness Sylvie's luck magic in process. Usually she gave me a charm that she'd already crafted, but it wasn't usual for me to be present when she created them.

The tree trunk trembled. Blood oozed around the shard. Tinsel's scream rent the air, then the spirit was abruptly silent. Sylvie turned to me with raised eyebrows.

I let out a breath. "He knows this is going to be painful. But the agony he suffers every day is unbearable. He'll endure if there's a chance this might break the curse."

Sylvie winced. "Okay. I hate that I'm causing him pain, but I'll proceed."

She took out another shard from her bag. "*Shatter.*"

Another scream. Another shard and spellword. Another scream. And on and on until I could hardly bear to keep watching. The tree trembled, blood covering the bark. Tinsel wasn't the only spirit who was suffering from my sister's spell. Mist-like forms had appeared around the tree—a dozen of them. The other elf spirits wailed and thrashed as Sylvie worked her magic.

The mirrored shards were embedded in a starburst pattern, and as Sylvie inserted the last one, they all glowed blue and gold. I felt the magic of the curse shift and weaken. The mirror shards snipped tiny threads of the elf queen's spell, and slowly it began to unravel. I caught my breath, afraid to say anything in case I jinxed the whole thing.

"*Shatter, shatter, shatter,*" Sylvie chanted. The press of her magic began to feel strained, labored. A bead of sweat rolled down her forehead and cheek. Her hands trembled and she clenched them into fists at her sides.

The unraveling slowed. I opened my senses and felt some of the elven spirits slip free. One. Three. Five. Eight.

Go. Go. I silently urged them. Tinsel would be the last to leave, and probably the hardest to free, but I knew he was thrilled that some of his friends were slipping through the weakening curse to their afterlife.

The unraveling spell halted and I felt it tremble. A few more spirits slipped through the bounds, then I felt the magic in the air change. Sylvie gasped and the mirror shards fell to dust, the curse back in place and stronger than it had been before.

"I'm so sorry." She turned to me and ran a shaky hand over her forehead. "I'm absolutely tapped out. I can't believe how powerful that spell was. I gave it everything I had, but just couldn't break it."

"You weakened it enough to free all the elves except Tinsel." I closed my eyes and felt the cursed elf's emotions. His torture had increased tenfold, but he was thrilled that the others had managed to escape.

Sylvie gave me a weak smile. "I'll try again another time. Maybe if I bring Eshu with me, together we can break the curse."

If she brought Eshu with her, there was a good chance the curse wouldn't be the only thing broken. I had no doubt that the trickster could free Tinsel, but in the process he'd probably end up leveling the mountain and killing us all.

"I won't give up either," I told my sister. My vow wasn't just to Sylvie and the werewolves, it was to Tinsel as well. I wouldn't give up. No matter how long it took, I'd eventually free him.

I turned to tell the werewolves it was safe to come forward, then caught sight of something out of the corner of my eye.

"Down," I shouted, pulling Sylvie to the ground with me.

A blaze of green light shot through the air right where our heads had just been, then bounced off the trees at the perimeter of the compound. The werewolves yelped and snarled, ducking down for cover, but the light didn't leave the circle of trees. It didn't harm the trees either. Taking that as a good sign, I eased to my knees, watching as the green light slowed then pivoted to form six-foot-tall oval next to the cursed tree.

Sylvie sucked in a breath and stood, pulling me to my feet. "It's a portal."

It was. And I had a good idea who was on the other side. "Should we run?" I asked her, even though I wasn't sure where we could go that we'd be safe from the elf queen.

Sylvie pushed her shoulders back. "Hell no, we shouldn't run. This is Accident. We're Perkins witches. We've blessed and warded this land, and *she* is a trespasser here."

A trespasser who assaulted our residents, who killed and cursed them on our land, on our watch. I pushed my shoulders back as well, my fear vanishing. This queen might be an ancient being with untold power, but I was a Perkins witch, and I would not retreat on my own land.

The green portal shimmered, and a being of light stepped through. The light coalesced, and before us stood a willowy woman about five feet tall. Her golden hair was styled in an intricate up-do and adorned with emeralds and white flowers that smelled like honey and wintergreen. Her eyes were abnormally large and as green as the gems in her hair. I stared at her, thinking she looked like a manga character, then shifted my gaze to her hands. Her long pointed nails were a pearly white—a match to the flowing dress she wore.

I'd grown up around the fae, so her carefully constructed appearance didn't startle or impress me. The glamour she wore swirled around my body, trying to force me to my knees in adoration of her otherworldly beauty, but we witches were immune to such things. I felt her power, but it didn't control me. I was pretty sure my immunity might not hold up if she brought out the big guns, though.

"Who dares try to break my spell?" she hissed, her weird eyes darting back and forth from Sylvie to me.

"I did," I chimed in before Sylvie could respond. I'd rather this elf's anger be focused on me since my sister was magically exhausted at the moment. "Decades ago you came uninvited to our lands, and dispensed judgement without even consulting us. These elves had our permission to live here, and your assault on our guests is an assault on us."

I wasn't sure why I decided it was a wise thing to go on the offense with the elven queen, but my boldness paid off. She blinked and tilted her head as she regarded me. "These elves stole what was mine and ran here to hide. Do you admit that you gave them asylum, knowing what they did?"

I mentally backpedaled, not wanting her to think our allowing the elves to live here was in any way an attack on her. I needed her to see that *we* were the aggrieved party—victims to her trespass, murder, and dark magic on our territory. That wouldn't fly if she thought we'd somehow shot first by knowingly harboring criminals.

"We had no idea that they stole from you. They arrived in Accident asking to live here as so many non-humans do, and we granted them land and resources. But your murdering and cursing their souls was done on our territory, without respect to our rule of law, and without any due process."

Clearly I'd been hanging around Cassie for too long. I was beginning to sound like a lawyer.

"They stole from me," the queen insisted. "Your laws do

not supersede ours, even here on this land you claim as your own."

"So if an elf were to steal from us, you would support us coming into your kingdom unannounced and without permission to kill them?" I asked.

She hissed. "No one comes to my kingdom without permission. Your laws and rules mean nothing to me. An elf who steals from humans or witches has broken no law. And elf who steals from their queen faces a punishment worse than death."

Logic wasn't getting anywhere with this woman. She saw herself as above us all, and none of my comparisons would convince her she'd done wrong.

If she had taken the elves back to her kingdom for punishment, we never would have known anything about their suffering. But she'd left them here, left their spirits to haunt our land with their pained cries. I had to think of some way to convince her to break the curse and release Tinsel.

I took a breath, and tried once more to explain our viewpoint. "You disrespected our rules. We may have supported you if you'd come to us, but you delivered justice on *our* lands without any respect for our rules. Because of that, we are absolutely within our rights to work to break your curse and free these souls. The curse is on *our* land. Their souls are haunting *our* mountain. You did not take the thieves back to your land for punishment, you cursed them here. You left them here. On our land. We have every right to free cursed souls who are on the lands we claim as our own."

"I punished those who stole from me. I had every right to do that no matter if they were here or in my lands. But you have released them." She took a step towards me. "You let all but one of them go. For that, you will pay."

"No, she will not."

I couldn't hide my surprise at the voice behind me.

Sylvie and I both turned to see Cassie walking out from the treeline. My eldest sister came to a stop beside me. "The Perkins witches have protected those who live in Accident for hundreds of years. This is our home. We will defend it from any who seek to attack us or our land."

The queen glanced from her to the others, then at the werewolves.

"Seven witches rule this place—and we have enormous power," Cassie continued. "Six of us have infernal mates. If one witch can nearly undo your curse, imagine what all seven of us plus our lovers can do. Then imagine those who would assist us—the trolls and fairies, the shifters, Valkyries and vampires, sylphs and giants, gargoyles and harpies. There are wulvers and dryads, a cyclops and a satyr. There is a dragon and a chimera. You will not win against us."

The queen sneered. "Your magic is nothing compared to mine."

"Try us," Cassie snapped.

Oh no. My eldest sister was known for her temper, and I absolutely didn't want her to land us all in the middle of a war with the elf queen.

"How about we compromise instead?" I suggested before the two of them started setting things on fire. "There are things you want, and there are things we want. I'm sure we can come to a non-violent solution here."

The elf queen hesitated, her eyes on me. "Go on."

The fae loved a good bargain, and it was best to start out with a ton of extravagant demands that would be whittled down to something more reasonable with negotiation. But I wasn't in the mood to barter for hours with this woman.

"How about if we locate the item that was stolen from you and return it. In exchange, you break your curse, free Tinsel from any further punishment and allow his soul passage to the afterlife. You also do no harm to any of us in or out of Accident, nor send anyone to harm us. You never return to Accident again, or the human lands."

The queen smiled, revealing rows of sharp teeth. "Bring me the Everbloom and I won't curse everyone in this town."

Yeah. No.

"We will find and bring you the Everbloom, and you will not curse anyone in this town. You will free Tinsel, breaking the curse and letting him go unhindered to his afterlife. You will never come here again, nor send anyone to harm us in or out of Accident, or the humans."

It was basically the same thing I'd asked for the first time, but I couldn't find any room to budge in my request. This was exhausting playing these word games with her, but I knew more than Tinsel's wellbeing was riding on this.

She looked at her nails for a moment. "Bring me the Everbloom and I won't curse the town or attack you, but I'm not setting this thief free."

"If we offer you a magical item in addition to the Everbloom, will you agree to break the curse and set Tinsel free?" I asked, desperate to help the elf.

Her eyes shone with greed, and I knew I'd found her weak spot.

"If the magical item pleases me and I accept it, then I will break the curse and set the thief free," she announced. "You have forty-eight hours, then our deal is off. I will leave this portal open for you to bring me the Everbloom and the gift."

Without waiting for a reply her form dissolved into a column of gold sparks, then vanished, leaving the green oval of light.

# CHAPTER 18

BABYLON

"*H*ow did you know we were here?" I asked Cassie once the elf queen was gone.

What I really wanted to know was how she'd managed to show up at exactly the right moment. My eldest sister was a powerful witch, but she wasn't omniscient.

Sylvie shot me a guilty look. "I called her. I just wanted to give her a heads-up that we were trying to break the curse. Just in case the whole mountain crashed down, or we all turned into newts, or something."

I frowned, not sure if Sylvie had been worried that her magic might produce the unintended and disastrous results, or if there would be a backlash from the curse being broken. Probably the latter. None of us had loads of experience with fae magic, and zero with the elven brand of fae magic. It had been wise of Sylvie to warn Cassie of what we were doing, and I felt like a fool for not thinking of that myself.

"I didn't come up here to micromanage you or anything," Cassie told me. "Honestly, I didn't intend to come up here at all until the wards went off. I had to use a spell that Lucian helped me craft. Damned near teleported'myself into the middle of the creek."

I swung my head around to look at Cassie. "The wards went off? If the elf queen's portal triggered the wards this time, then it probably did when she came here to curse the others. Isadora was Accident's witch when the elves first arrived, but seventy years later, Grandma would have been the witch in charge of Accident. She must have known."

Sylvie's eyes widened. "And if she knew, there would be a note in her journal."

"That note might not be of any use," Cassie warned us. "Grandma wouldn't have been able to teleport. By the time she drove up to Savior Mountain to check on the ward alarm, the queen and the elves living here were most likely gone."

"She probably thought the elves returning home trigger the ward," I mused. "Maybe that's how the rumor that they'd left started."

Cassie shrugged. "Maybe. It wouldn't have been a perimeter ward, since the queen probably appeared right in the middle of the settlement, just like she did this time. Residents sometimes trigger the overall protective wards with their magic. Clearly opening up a big-ass portal on the mountain triggers them as well."

"The wards of thirty years ago weren't quite as good as the ones we have now," Sylvie cautioned.

She was right. Bronwyn took care of the perimeter and safety wards, and she was unusually talented when it came to that sort of magic.

"I still want to check both Isadora's and Grandma's journals," I told them. "Just in case there's something useful there."

Cassie nodded. "It's a good thing today is Sunday. We'll all be together for dinner tonight, and we can fill everyone in and strategize. Bronwyn is going to need to pull out all the stops on creating a beautiful, enchanted gift. We need to present the queen with something she'll absolutely love—love enough to let that poor elf free."

"And we need to find this Everbloom," Sylvie reminded us.

"I'll try to communicate with Tinsel later," I said. "With the other elves free, he might be more willing to risk giving the flower back to the queen."

"He doesn't have much to lose," Cassie said. "This is his only chance to be free from an eternity of suffering."

There was so much riding on this whole thing. Tinsel. The town of Accident. All of our residents here. And we only had forty-eight hours.

Clinton came toward us. "I heard what that elf woman said. We'll help. We've gotten to know this mountain pretty well over the last few months. If you can get a description of this flower, or any idea of where it might be, then I can turn the whole pack loose to search."

"Thank you. We'll definitely take you up on that offer," I told him.

The werewolves cordoned off the area with the log with caution tape, and I gave both Sylvie and Cassie a ride back to town, dropping Sylvie off at her house before going to Cassie.

I left my eldest sister prepping for tonight's dinner and headed up the stairs into the attic. It was warm up there. The heat rose through the two floors below and counteracted the chill weather that was moving in. I sorted through boxes until I found the one I wanted, then sat in an old rocking chair and began to read.

With only a vague idea of when the elves arrived, I started with one of Isadora's journals from a hundred years ago and flipped through scores of entries about town festivals, sanitation systems, and the usual issues with the werewolf pack. Finally I found a brief few paragraphs that mentioned the elves.

*The wards chimed today at 1:36 this afternoon in the wilds of Savior Mountain. No one lives there currently, but the shifters do occasionally hunt there and the fairy-folk hold festivals in the watershed area, so I was not alarmed. Sometimes their magic triggers these wards—an issue I've been trying unsuccessfully to fix for the last ten years. After I finished my baking, I put on my boots and made my way there, hoping I did not disturb one of the fairy-folk festivals, as that makes them grumpy. Imagine my surprise when I arrived to see a newly cleared area and houses! The place appeared to be vacant, but my amulet glowed, sensing magic and the presence of more than just me and the animals in the woods. I cast a spell, and it told me these were newcomers, the likes of which Accident had never seen before.*

*I called out a greeting, and they came forth. There were thirteen small fairylike creatures. The leader's name is Tinsel and he informed me that they were elves, come here to live in peace. I welcomed them, let them know the rules of Accident, and said that they should feel free to come see me with any questions or concerns they might have.*

*They all seemed cautious and wary. Afraid. I know newcomers are often overwhelmed, so I left them in peace and intend to check back with them in a few weeks.*

I paged further ahead in the journal, noting that while Isadora made several visits to the elves over the next few months, they continued to seem afraid and to prefer their solitude. Any offer to participate in town events or meet the others was met with a polite but firm refusal. Finally Isadora stopped visiting them, trusting that they'd let her know if they needed anything or changed their mind about meeting the townfolk.

The whole thing sounded fishy to me, but I could see how

my great grandmother would not have noticed any red flags. The werewolf pack back then was also reclusive and isolated on their mountain territory. Heck, the werewolf clan had still been that way most of my life. It was only recently, after the pack had split, that werewolves were more frequently seen in town, and a brave few outside of Accident in the human world. The joy of Accident was that the residents could live the way they wanted with only a few rules to abide by. They could walk about in their natural forms and perform their magic without fear of persecution from the humans. It was the utopia that our ancestor, Temperance Perkins, had founded when she'd narrowly escaped the witch trials with her life, and each successive generation of witches had dedicated our lives to protecting the town and the residents.

I couldn't blame Isadora for not digging into the background of the newcomers and discovering their secrets. It wasn't the way we did things in Accident.

It took me hours, but in my Grandmother's journals I found the final entry about the elves just as the smell of pork ribs permeated the attic.

*A ward was triggered tonight about six o'clock. It wasn't until later that I realized it had come from the exact same spot on Savior Mountain the elves had set off when they arrived back in my mother's day. I've spent the last two decades working on adjusting the wards not to occasionally flare when a resident does magic, but haven't been successful in correcting the problem. Because of this, I wasn't particularly concerned. Wards are triggered once or twice a month since I've been the head witch, and none of those has been cause for alarm. This time I was in the middle of crafting a set of charms, and normally I would have put off investigating until the next day, but in the seventy years the elves have lived here, they've never set off the ward to my knowledge aside from during their arrival. If this had been their magic during a festival or celebration, then it would have happened in the past as well.*

Thinking it might be a group of their friends arriving to join them, I wasn't particularly concerned, but something worried me about the breach in the wards, so I put aside the charms and headed for Savior Mountain.

As the elves never leave the area they now call home, the roads up the mountain had become incredibly overgrown and difficult to traverse. I traveled on horseback, but sweet Aspen still had to go around fallen trees and thick patches of brush, as well as up and down a few steep and muddy banks. Luckily the sun doesn't set until after nine in the evening, but I still found myself arriving at eight and worried about heading home in the dark.

There were no lights, no scents, and no sign of activity when I finally rode into the compound. I dismounted and tied Aspen to a tree, calling out to the elves. Mother had said they'd always appeared fearful the times she'd come to see them, so finding the area empty didn't seem unusual. None of the elves answered my call. None of the firepits were warm and the houses were empty of all belongings. I activated my amulet and it told me that besides the woodland animals, Aspen, and myself, there were no other beings on the mountain.

The elves were gone. Their personal items were gone. Given the state of the road, I doubted they'd suddenly decided after all these years to relocate closer to town. The signal from the ward was as Mother had described from when they arrived, so my assumption was that they had all left Accident and returned to their homeland.

I'll admit I was a bit irritated that they had left without telling me their intentions. I'd wasted nearly two hours coming up here, and would waste another two heading back—in the dark as well. Plus I wasted the six charms that I had to abandon mid-spell.

But everyone in Accident has their own ideas of civility and manners, so I brushed off my skirts, let go of my annoyance, and headed back home. Thankfully Aspen and I made better time, and were down the mountain before the sun had completely set for the night.

DEBRA DUNBAR

I closed the journal and carefully packed it away, returning the box to its original location. I'd been blaming my grandmother for the fact that a dozen elves and Tinsel had suffered under a curse, right in Accident and under our very noses, but reading her journal confirmed that she wasn't at fault.

The elves hadn't confided in her or anyone else. They hadn't made friends. For seven decades they'd remained isolated on their mountain. I didn't blame Grandma for thinking they'd just gone back to their homeland and forgetting about the whole thing. If there had been signs of a struggle or anything suspicious, she would have investigated. But all she'd seen was a group of empty houses and cold hearths.

Grandma wasn't at fault for what happened, but I was still honor bound to ensure the curse Tinsel suffered under was broken and he was set free. I'd locate this Everbloom and take both it and a gift of Bronwyn's crafting to the elf queen. I'd do everything in my power to make sure she broke the curse.

Then I'd come back, find a way to give Maude a second life, and hope that none of us ever saw the elf queen again.

# CHAPTER 19

## HADES

*I* knocked on the door of the house, oddly nervous. Babylon's sister lived in an old house that had been clearly added onto throughout the generations. It was eclectic, and felt well-loved. But as warm and welcoming as the house was, I had my concerns about how Babylon's family would feel about me. I knew humans were very protective of the youngest in their families, and I was sure I'd be subjected to some intense scrutiny.

The door opened and a tall, auburn-haired woman stood in the entrance. I saw the resemblance right away.

"You must be Hades." She opened the door wider. "I'm Sylvie. Come on in."

I entered to find the large open-space living and dining room packed with people. A long table sat near a doorway that I assumed led to the kitchen. Glancing around, I recognized all of the males present except one of them.

"I'm Aaron." The red-haired man put out his hand.

"Hades." I shook hands, noting that he too bore a family resemblance. Ah, this must be the cousin Babylon had mentioned.

Sylvie grabbed me by the arm and hauled me around the room, introducing me to everyone. I've got a good memory for details, but I knew I'd never be able to remember their names at this first meeting—or tell the two women apart who were clearly twins. After the introductions, Aaron brought me into the kitchen where Babylon was busy helping yet another sister assemble a salad. Lucien peered at me from around the refrigerator door.

"Hades! Want a beer?" he asked.

"Absolutely." I needed something stronger than a beer. Babylon's family was huge and loud, and I found myself more than a little overwhelmed by it all.

"Don't worry if you can't remember everyone's names. I can't remember their names and I grew up with them," Aaron said as Lucien handed both him and me a beer.

"Ha ha ha." Babylon walked up and gave me a quick kiss on the cheek that made my heart speed up. She had a set of onyx earrings on that were pretty against her red hair. I caught a glimmer of magic, and was surprised to notice it wasn't the witch magic that infused the entire house, but something different.

"I like these," I told her as I touched one of the dangling onyx and silver drops.

"Thanks." She laughed and shook her head, sending her bright red hear and the earrings in motion. "I kind of got conned into buying them this morning. Some of the fairies in town own a jewelry shop."

Ah. Fae magic. I didn't have much opportunity to encounter fae, so I hadn't recognized their work at first.

"How was your day?" Babylon asked, taking my hand in hers.

"Unsuccessful." I forced a smile to my face. Would she ever confess to me what she'd done? I hoped that she'd trust me, but I couldn't blame her for keeping this from me when we'd only just met each other last night.

"No one seems to have any idea what happened to that lost soul," I continued. "I've spoken to necromancers both alive and dead. I've interviewed the other souls who were taken but returned. I'm running out of time to find that soul. The angels are getting impatient, and are still accusing hell of stealing her."

"Those angels are just looking for any excuse to fight," Eshu added. He seemed disturbingly excited by the prospect.

I, on the other hand, was absolutely *not* excited. I hated fighting. If there was going to be a war between heaven and hell, I was going to have to invoke the hazardous duty clauses in my contracts.

"There's *another* lost soul?" Lucien asked me before turning to one of the sisters. "Did you adopt another squirrel, Addy?"

She stuck out her tongue at Lucien. "No, I haven't. Is there another soul missing from hell, Ty?"

Typhon shook his head. "Not on my watch. And not that I've heard of."

"It's not one of hell's souls, it's one of heaven's," I explained. "Lucien, I might need to ask you to intervene on this one because they think hell stole her. A bunch of souls from hell, purgatory and heaven all vanished at the same time, and all of them returned except for one from heaven. They were all the same family, and had lived on a farm near here when they were alive."

The eldest sister dropped a pan, then swore as she bent down to pick it up.

She knew. Lucien and the others didn't seem to realize that Babylon was involved, but Cassie knew. I looked over at Adrienne and saw her tilt her head. Then her eyes widened and she shot Babylon a panicked look.

Babylon frowned at her, giving a slight shake of her head before she turned to me. "Why don't you and Lucien talk about that after dinner. We're just about to eat."

We all made our way into the dining room where a heated discussion broke out about who was going to have to eat at the kitchen table.

"We need to discuss something urgent that effects Accident," Cassie said. "Aaron, Eshu, Xavier, and Hades can eat in the kitchen."

"I ate in the kitchen last Sunday," Aaron complained. "And the Sunday before."

"It's Hades first dinner here," Babylon argued. "It's rude to make him eat in the kitchen on his first Sunday dinner."

"I'm good," Eshu announced as he headed through the doorway. "I'll be closer to the oven and those amazing pork ribs. And I can grab a slice of the key lime pie before anyone else."

"Don't you touch that pie," Sylvie shouted after him.

"Okay. Eshu, Xavier, Lucien, and Hadur." Cassie waved her hand. "Go. Go. Before the food gets cold."

There was a lot of grumbling, and several comments about how those of us in the dining room needed to speak loudly so those in the kitchen could hear. We sat down, and for a while there was silence as everyone feasted on the ribs, roasted carrots, salad, and fresh sourdough rolls.

Finally Cassie pushed her plate away with a sigh and spoke up. "I hate to bring this up during family dinner, but we only have forty-eight hours to resolve this issue. One hundred years ago a group of elves came here and lived on Savior Mountain in complete isolation from the rest of Accident. Thirty years ago they vanished and everyone thought they had just packed up and gone home."

"Until a tree fell during a storm up on Savior Mountain two weeks ago, and the werewolves started seeing ghosts,"

Babylon added. "Those elves didn't go home. The elven queen came to Accident, murdered them all, and cursed their souls because one of them had stolen an item from her."

The others all exclaimed, including the ones in the kitchen. Some were angry that such an act had been done here and had gone unnoticed. Others focused on the elves' plight. I watched Babylon as she told us all about the bargain she'd struck with the elf queen that would hopefully free the remaining cursed elf, and avoid a war with the elves. My heart swelled as I listened to her. She was smart, passionate, and truly cared about others—even this elf who had lived and died before she'd been born. It reinforced my desire to protect her somehow from any ramifications for what she'd done. Maybe her keeping Maude Hoffman's soul was an accident, or she had a good reason for what she'd done. I wanted to give her the benefit of the doubt. And I wanted to help her not just in that situation, but in this one with the elf and the vengeful queen.

"I've got the perfect gift," the sister introduced to me as Bronwyn announced. "It's a little silver bird, enameled and decorated with gems. It sings whenever you wish it to. Any song. I should be able to complete it by tomorrow morning if I work through the night."

"Can you show it to Mirabelle? Just to make sure it's something that the elf queen would like," Babylon said. "I know fae are sensitive to iron. I just want to double check that nothing about the design or specific gems causes offense." She put a hand on my arm. "Are you free tomorrow? I'd really like it if you went up to Savior Mountain with me and helped look for the Everbloom."

"Of course." I put my hand over hers and squeezed gently before letting go, thrilled that she was including me.

"I'll be the one to deliver the flower and the gift to the elf queen." Cassie held up a hand as Lucien popped out of the kitchen to protest. "I know, I know. But I'm the strongest witch among us. If she attacks or decides to hold me hostage, I've got the best chance of fighting her and getting away."

"No you don't," Babylon argued. "One of us will never be able to stand against her. And if she captures you then attacks Accident, we're screwed. You need to be here to fight if she comes after the town."

"Babylon's right," Adrienne chimed in. "I'll go instead."

"No you won't. I will," Babylon informed her. "*I'm* the one who made the deal. I'm the one who took the blame for the spell that allowed twelve of the elves to escape the curse. She won't deal if I'm not the one delivering the goods. Besides, I'm the only one who will know for sure if she truly releases Tinsel."

"And it sounds as if the queen is unaware of your actual abilities," I reminded Babylon. "You took claim for the attempt to break the curse. She has no idea that you are a necromancer. It could work to your advantage."

Most everyone was afraid of necromancers. I'd seen this in hell where both the demons and the other souls gave them plenty of space and respect. Even when they were being tortured, it was always done with the utmost courtesy. Of all the magical abilities, necromancy was the most feared.

Instead of being bolstered by my words, Babylon frowned.

"Are there dead in the elven kingdom? Do they die? Does anyone die? Threatening her with an army of animated corpses isn't going to work if there aren't any corpses to animate."

Cassie shrugged. "I've never seen a fairy die. I've always assumed they were incredibly long-lived, or even immortal as far as aging and disease went. But this queen murdered thirteen elves and cursed their spirits, so I'm assuming there are probably murdered corpses in their kingdom at the very least."

Babylon turned to me again. "I just thought of something! You said you designed more than just heaven, hell, and purgatory. Did you have anything to do with the design and creation of the elven lands?"

I shook my head, hating to let her down. "Unfortunately, no. I only design places where the dead reside. I mean, living beings are there as well, but the places function is to serve as a resting place for souls. There is an afterlife for the fae that I helped build, but the kingdom for their living isn't something I had a hand in."

She sighed. "Drat. I'd hoped you'd know about a backdoor or an emergency exit or something."

I did know something that would allow her to escape the elven world, or anywhere, but I was afraid to suggest it. We barely knew each other, and while this witch stirred my heart, I knew I needed to take things slow.

I'd rushed a relationship before, and it had ended in disaster. I didn't want to make the same mistake with Babylon.

Babylon ran a hand through her hair. "I really screwed this up. Now the entire town has been threatened and we have to worry that this queen will find a way to attack us in spite of our deal."

"What that queen did was wrong," Cassie insisted. "If we let her get away with murdering and cursing those elves, then we'd be derelict in our duty as the protectors of Accident."

"Besides, if we failed to right that wrong and protect those who were cursed, then how could any of the residents trust us to protect and help them?" Ophelia asked. "We cannot turn our backs on any of our residents."

"If she wiggles out of her deal and attacks us, we'll be ready," Glenda said.

"All of us," Adrienne agreed. "The townfolk will take up arms to protect Accident as well. They'll fight by our sides."

"And I'll call upon the minions of hell to assist," Lucien vowed.

"We've got this," Cassie insisted. "All of us. Together."

"Me, too." I looked at Babylon, knowing I'd do anything to help her, anything to protect her—even if it meant risking my heart once more.

# CHAPTER 20

## BABYLON

*E*arly the next morning I sat in the diner, gripping my mug of coffee and waiting for Hades. He wasn't late, it was me that was half an hour early and trying to work up the nerve to tell him about Maude. I really liked this guy, but this secret was eating me up inside.

He must think I was a total hot mess with my crazy family, the cursed elves, and a potential war with an elf queen. If I added Maude to that mess, he'd run screaming. And if he didn't run screaming, he'd probably just walk away and never see me again. I knew he was looking for Maude. I knew what was riding on this whole thing. But I just couldn't make myself tell him.

I didn't want to see that look on his face—the one where he was disgusted at what I'd done, disappointed that I hadn't fessed up to it right away, angry that I hadn't been honest with him from the very start.

Why had I invited him to come today? What was it about me that I thought spending a whole day tromping around a mountain looking for a stolen elven item would be romantic? Plus, I'd need to contact Tinsel again to try to narrow down where to look for the Everbloom. There would be blood and screaming. Not romantic at all. Nope.

Maybe I wouldn't have to tell him about Maude. He'd see my freaky magic in action and witness Tinsel's agony over the curse, and this relationship would be over before it truly started.

The door chimed and Hades walked in, casually dressed in jeans and a black T-shirt, a leather jacket slung over one shoulder. My breath lodged in my throat then I exhaled with a whoosh. Wow, he looked good. Really good. I didn't want him to walk away from me.

I needed to tell him. Today. I couldn't put it off any longer.

Hades smiled at me and made his way to my table, sliding in across from me. "I wasn't sure what to wear to go hunting for an Everbloom. I assumed it might involve some digging?"

I waved the waiter over to fill a mug with coffee for Hades. "Possibly. I'd supposed this thing was a flower, but Tinsel might have buried it. Heck, for all I know, it needs to be buried in the ground to do its magic."

"It might not even look like a flower," he commented.

"It could look like a rock or a leaf," I agreed.

"Or a clump of dirt," he suggested.

"A stick. A petrified chunk of deer poo." I sighed. Hopefully Tinsel would be able to give us information on not just where the Everbloom was, but how to recognize it when we saw it. "Even if we have exact coordinates, how are we going to know which stick or leaf or chunk of poo is the Everbloom?"

"I can sense magic," he informed me, as if this was no big deal.

"*All* magic?" We all had the ability to sense certain types of magic, but without an enchanted object, like something Bronwyn could create, neither me nor my sisters could feel or recognize all the different types of magic even in Accident.

"All magic." He sipped his coffee. "But my ability to sense residual magic isn't quite as fine-tuned."

"So if I animated a dead bird then returned it to the grave, how long could you sense my magic on the body?" I asked.

He smiled. "You are incredibly powerful. I believe I could probably sense the necromantic magic for a week or so. I would recognize the magic as yours as well."

I caught my breath, wondering if he'd caught my magic on the souls who'd returned to hell, or the graves at Rita's farm. It had been two weeks since I'd raised the zombies, so I was hoping that had been enough time for my magic to dissipate.

"Do you feel my magic even when I'm not casting a spell?" I asked.

"Yes," he replied without hesitation. "It's not just residual magic that clings to you after you've done a magical working. You're a witch. You're a necromancer. I can see the magic that's a part of who you are. And there was that dead opossum you animated and put in the backseat that first night when we went to the Disco Diner."

I laughed, remembering the opossum. "So you sense my sisters' magic as well? Lucien's? Nash's? Everyone here in the diner?"

"In the diner?" He grinned. "Three gnomes, two harpies, an ifrit, two pixies, a goblin, a sylph, and two mermaids. There's a shifter in the kitchen."

My mouth dropped open, amazed. This guy was as good as one of Bronwyn's amulets, and he didn't need a magical recharge every few weeks.

"You'll be able to sense the Everbloom?" Maybe I wouldn't need to communicate with Tinsel and cause him additional pain. If Hades could hone in on the artifact like a

DEBRA DUNBAR

divining rod, it would save us a lot of time as well. I'd invited him along because I wanted his company, and never thought that he might have abilities that could make the hunt for the Everbloom easier.

"I probably won't be able to step foot on the mountain and know right where it is," he warned. "From what you said, it's been deactivated with no living elves around. So whatever magical signature it has would be subtle. But I will definitely recognize that it's not a normal flower, or stick, or clump of mud. And I'll pick up elven magical signatures from the portal and the curse, so I'd also be able to tell the Everbloom from, say, a ring of mushrooms that maybe the fairies have enchanted."

So, not quite as easy as I'd hoped when he first told me about his abilities, but it was reassuring to know he'd be able to recognize the elven artifact no matter what form it might be in.

We finished our coffee, discussing the best ways to conduct the search, then I drove up to the werewolf compound. Our wolf escorts ran alongside my car for the last half mile, yipping and howling to signal our arrival. Clinton came out as we were parking. I got out and introduced Hades. The alpha werewolf dismissed the others and the three of us walked together to the cordoned off lumberyard.

"I don't like this, Babylon," Clinton told me. "I worry about you going to meet that elf queen in her territory. There's not as many ghost sightings now that a dozen of them have been set free from the curse. I might be able to convince the other werewolves to stay here with the bleeding, screaming, haunted tree."

I appreciated his offer, but we both knew his pack would flee from Savior Mountain if I didn't do something about the bleeding, screaming, haunted tree. In addition, that bleeding, screaming, haunted tree was Tinsel, and I couldn't just give up and let him suffer under a curse for all of eternity when there was something I could do to help him.

And in the end, I'd struck a deal with the elf queen. One didn't just ignore a bargain made with fae. If I didn't deliver the goods, Clinton's werewolf pack and the rest of Accident would have a whole lot more to deal with than a screaming, bleeding, haunted tree. They'd have war.

"I need to do this," I assured the alpha. Then I turned to Hades. "You might want to stand back with the werewolves while I try to talk to Tinsel. It's…unsettling."

"I designed hell. Every day I walk by souls being punished. I'm okay with unsettling," he told me. "Besides, there must be something I can do to help. Set up candles? Help draw sigils? Hold the incense?"

His offer gave me an idea. I dug around in my bag and pulled out a vial of dirt. "Here. Hold this. I've got something I want to try after I talk to Tinsel.

Hades looked at the vial. "Grave dirt?"

I nodded. "The elf queen can tell when someone's messing with the curse. I don't think she'll interfere if I'm just speaking with Tinsel. I mean, it is in her best interest for us to find the Everbloom so we can return it to her. But if I'm holding that grave dirt while I'm working my magic, and she somehow senses it…"

"Then she might think the bargain is off and show up with an army." Hades eyed the vial again. "But a bystander not actively involved in your spell and holding a container of dirt isn't something she'll be bothered about."

I nodded. "I doubt her reach goes any further than the curse, Tinsel, and the log. She probably won't even know you're there."

"Is there anything else I can do to help?" Hades asked.

I glanced over at the green portal, wondering if the

queen came through to snatch me, or harm me, what he could do. Other than teleport between here and the afterlife structures he'd design, and his ability to sense magic, what could Hades do? Did he have any defensive magic? Any offensive magic?

"Get a good read on the elf magic," I finally said. "The queen's curse, Tinsel's magic if you can sense it, and anything else that feels similar. I'm going to really need your help in finding the Everbloom. I doubt Tinsel is going to tell me the exact coordinates of where it is. The queen is listening and he won't want her to know."

Plus, in typical fae fashion he'd cloak it all in metaphor or riddles or something.

I refreshed the chalk runes, lit four candles and cast a protective circle with both Hades and myself on the inside and Clinton watching from about fifty feet away. Then I took out my athame and sunk it into the rotted bark of the tree as I called out for Tinsel. Blood welled up around the knife, and I heard the elf scream in pain.

"Tinsel, we've struck a bargain with the elf queen. I need to know where the Everbloom is hidden so I can return it to her."

"She'll never set me free. Never," he moaned.

"We made a bargain," I told him, but the nature of my deal with the elf queen worried me. I was exchanging the Everbloom for the safety of Accident. It was Bronwyn's gift that I hoped would be enticing enough to secure Tinsel's freedom. But I'd need the Everbloom first. I wanted the elf queen to have her artifact back and have a face-saving way for her to reverse the curse.

"Doomed. Cursed. Forever," he cried.

"This is our one chance to free you. We need to know where the Everbloom is, otherwise you will be cursed forever. This is our *one* chance," I repeated.

There was a long silence, then another pained scream from the log.

"Those who know me, who lived and walked beside me will find the Everbloom," he said, his voice weak. "Those who seek with a pure heart and a love for all things living and dead will find the Everbloom."

Tinsel barely got the last word out before he began screaming again. I waved for Hades and he upended the grave dirt onto the log.

"Ashes to ashes, dust to dust. Rest, your soul free as your body returns to the earth," I said.

The dirt on the log smoked then caught fire with a shower of sparks. I reached out with my awareness and knew that although Tinsel was still cursed, I'd managed to lessen his pain.

The green portal flared and a series of darts flew from it, aimed directly at us. Before I could react, Hades threw his hands out and the air shimmered. The darts vanished, and the portal was now surrounded by that distorted, flickering air.

"Nice work." I took a step closer to Hades, unnerved to think we'd been half a second from being pierced by those darts—darts that most definitely had probably carried horrible magic. "What happened to the darts?"

"They're currently in a lava pit in hell." He grimaced. "I didn't stop to think about whether they were magicked or not."

My eyes widened as I thought about some lava pit suddenly exploding.

He sighed. "I guess I'll have to deal with that later. There might need to be some emergency repairs in the sixth circle."

"Will the demons and damned souls be okay?" I had no idea what the magic on those darts might do when they hit a lava pit in hell.

"Oh, I'm sure they're okay." He shrugged. "Not much can kill a demon, and the damned souls are already dead. Plus, I doubt whatever was on those darts was lethal. The queen wants her Everbloom and is curious about the gift. She wouldn't kill you and cut off her chance of getting both."

He had a point.

We started walking toward Clinton and the cluster of werewolves who'd gathered at the edge of the lumberyard.

"Did Tinsel say anything that might help us find the Everbloom?" Hades asked.

"In between his screams?" I winced, thinking of the curse. "I know that was bad. I hate that you had to see it...or hear it."

He stopped walking and faced me. "Babylon, I know many people, probably even some of your family, find your magic unsettling. Others find it disgusting. I don't. You are doing everything within your power to help that poor elf. You're going to break this curse and set him free. I find that admirable. And I see your magic as a beautiful thing."

"Thank you." It was the first time anyone had ever called my magic beautiful. And the thought that he saw Tinsel's pain as a horribly necessary evil so we could release this curse meant a lot to me.

"Do you have any idea what Tinsel may have meant?" he asked as we continued to walk. "Everyone that ever knew him is dead or back in his homeland. Did he mean that you know him well enough to find the Everbloom?"

"I think so," I mused. "As much as I can, anyway. I've spoken to Tinsel twice. I've read my family's journal entries about the elves. I've been—" Suddenly I stopped. "Wait. When we came up here to build the houses for the were-wolves, there were no existing structures. The elves vanished thirty years ago and the buildings were still here then. There should have been structures, even if they were crumbling and overgrown."

174

"Maybe their magic made them vanish without a trace within a certain amount of time?" Hades asked.

"Yeah, but..." I snapped my fingers. "The sugar maple grove! When the elf queen murdered and cursed the elves, she wouldn't have hauled them down the access road to that grove to do it, she would have killed them right where they stood—right in their village."

"So the elves didn't live in this spot," Hades commented. "Their village was where the sugar maple grove now stands."

"That's where we need to start," I said. "That's where those who knew Tinsel would have gone to find him. That's where he was even in death—until the storm brought the tree down and the werewolves brought the log here to their compound."

"Can we help?" Clinton asked.

I started to say no then changed my mind. "Any werewolf who thinks they might be able to pick up an elven scent left on an object thirty years ago, or sense an elven item can help us search the sugar maple grove. I don't want too many feet tramping around the area, but I could definitely use a few good noses."

Clinton gave me thumbs-up. "I've got two wolves who'll be perfect. I'll have them start on the perimeter of the grove while you two work in the middle."

"Wouldn't the Everbloom be right in the center of their village?" Hades asked. "It seems like the logical spot for the artifact that transformed the mountain into something more like their homeland."

"It does seem like the perfect place, but I'm sure the queen would have looked there first." I frowned. "It has to be close though. Tinsel said those who knew him, who lived and walked beside him would find it. So I'm thinking it's either in the spot where they had their compound, or near the compound in an area where the elves may have frequented."

Hades and I drove down to the spot where the tree had fallen, then made our way through some dense brush to where the sugar maple grove stood. While two werewolves sniffed around the trees, I looked around and tried to put myself in Tinsel's shoes. If I were a suspicious elf looking to hide an artifact but still wanting it close by, where would I put it?

"Babylon?" Hades waved me over. "Come see this."

I went, and he positioned me directly in front of him, hands on my shoulders. "Look at the branches of the trees."

I gasped. "It's a heart!"

Tinsel had said those who sought with a pure heart and a love for all things living and dead would find the Everbloom. I hadn't thought to take that statement literally, but here, right in front of me, was a heart. The branches of three sugar maple trees arched in the air, creating a heart-shape with their boughs.

Hades and I ran over and began searching the area around the heart. He took the ground, while I began examining the trees, remembering to look upward into the canopy of red and gold leaves. Not finding anything, I moved further away to where a stream angled through the rocky ground. The elves would have come this way for water. Perhaps Tinsel hid the Everbloom here.

I was so engrossed in searching that I fell over a burrow. Catching my fall before I ate dirt, I let out a curse as I stood. I was brushing off my pants when a huge badger shuffled out of the burrow. The thing looked annoyed and had some intimidatingly long claws, so I summoned a dozen dead spiders.

The badger squealed, transformed into human, and began to dance around.

"What the bloody hell, woman? Get these things off of me."

A shifter. A badger shifter. A very naked badger shifter with his substantial junk flopping around as he tried to get away from the undead spiders.

"Oh, sorry!" I dismissed the spiders, but the badger shifter seemed just as nervous about their little dead corpses as he had been when they'd been moving corpses.

Addy had said that there was a badger shifter living up on Savior Mountain near the werewolf compound. I just hadn't realized his sett was right here.

"For fuck's sake," he complained, wiping a hand over his body and eyeing the dead spiders on the ground. "I'm woken from a sound sleep by someone nearly putting a foot through the roof of my sett, and when I come out, I get attacked by zombie spiders. I hate spiders. Hate them dead just as much as living."

I remembered Addy telling me that badgers ate insects as well as earthworms and small mammals, but shifters weren't always exactly like their animal counterpart. Evidently this one was afraid of spiders.

"I'm so sorry." I went to brush one of the spider corpses off of him, but changed my mind when I realized that would put my hand dangerously close to the guy's dick. "I didn't recognize you and summoned the dead out of reflex when you came out of your sett. Your claws are large, and I just reacted."

"That isn't the only thing about me that's large." The badger swiveled his hips.

I glanced down, wishing I hadn't. The dude was huge—freakishly huge. As in, send-a-woman-to-the-hospital huge.

"Well, since I'm awake, I might as well get a bite to eat." He eyed my bag. "You wouldn't happen to have a roast or a chicken in there, would you?"

"No." I dug around in my bag, wondering if Maude had

thrown a snack or something in there that I could offer the guy.

"Beef jerky?" He walked close to peer over my shoulder into the bag. I felt something brush against my ass and absolutely didn't want to contemplate what it was.

"A granola bar?" I offered.

He wrinkled his nose. "Yuck. I'll just go grab some grubs. One of the reasons I built my sett here is because of those grubs."

"Babylon?" I turned to see Hades. His eyebrows shot up, no doubt because the man next to me was naked with his dick practically against my ass.

"Accidently tripped over a badger shifter's house," I explained. "You wouldn't happen to have a roast or some beef jerky would you?"

"No." He tilted his head. "A roast? Why do you need a roast?"

The badger shifter waved his hand. "Nevermind. Those grubs are my go-to snack. There's an endless supply of them. It's the weirdest thing, although you'd think I'd be used to weird things on this mountain."

I put the granola bar back in my bag and watched as the badger tore a chunk off a rotted log and pulled out a handful of grubs. Then I blinked in surprise as the missing piece of log magically reappeared.

"It's amazing," the shifter said, his mouth full. "You witches have the best magic."

That...that wasn't our magic. I took a step toward the log. It was dead, but teaming with life. Looking up and turning around, I realized the log was in a direct line from the sugar maple grove—right across from where the branches formed a heart.

"Hades!" I called out, hardly daring to hope that this

might be it. "Come here and see if you sense anything about this log."

He walked over then nodded. "Yes! It's absolutely under some sort of elven spell. The magic is very similar to that of the curse, but far older."

"It has to be the Everbloom." The artifact was working its magic on the log, but where exactly was it? Was the Everbloom the log itself? The grubs? I glanced over at the badger shifter in alarm, only to realize he hardly would have been eating portions of an elven artifact for years without knowing something was different about his favorite snack food.

"What's an Everbloom?" the shifter asked, his mouth full of grubs.

Hades explained it all while I knelt down to look at the log. It made sense. We'd come to the grove where those who knew Tinsel, who lived and walked with him resided. We walked through the "pure of heart" shape made by the trees. We found the spot where the living and the dead resided. Where was it?

*With a love for all things living and dead,* Tinsel had said. That was me. I equally loved the living and the dead. I walked with both. I embraced both. Reaching out with both hands, I closed my eyes and touched the log, trying to see with my inner sight. When I opened my eyes, the log and the grubs were gone, and cradled in my hands was a tiny glass orchid that sparkled with fae magic.

"Where? How?" Hades sputtered. "I didn't even sense it until just now. How did you find it?"

"I walk with the living and the dead," I explained as I got to my feet. "I think that's the power of the Everbloom. I believe it is a bridge across the veil, something that transcends life and death. I don't completely understand its magic, or how it can reproduce the magic of an elven home-land, but when I put my hands on the log, it came to me."

Was it a horrible coincidence that Tinsel had hidden the Everbloom in the form of a dead log, shielding and hiding its magic, and he'd suffered a similar fate in the queen's curse, entombed forever in a tree?

We'd found it. We'd found the Everbloom and were one step closer to freeing Tinsel. Clinton would be thrilled when I told him. As would Cassie. Now I would just make plans for tomorrow, and try one last time to resurrect Maude before I walked into the elven queen's homeland, perhaps never to leave.

And I needed to tell Hades about Maude. I couldn't delay that any longer.

"Where'd it go?" the badger shifter sputtered. "You nearly cave in my sett. You attack me with a bunch of dead spiders. And now you magic away my endless snack bar of grubs. You witches owe me. You owe me a roast. And a chicken. And a case of beef jerky."

And with that, he spun around, transformed back into a badger, and stomped back into his sett.

# CHAPTER 21

*W*e sat in the diner, munching on fried pickles with the Everbloom in a small box between us. The first thing I'd done after calling Cassie and telling Clinton had been to order a case of beef jerky to send to the badger shifter. Poor guy. It wasn't an endless supply of grubs, but hopefully it would serve as an apology for taking away his all-you-can-eat snack bar.

"I can't believe we found it so easily," Hades said, nudging the box toward me.

"I can't believe the elf queen didn't see it!" I exclaimed. It had been right there, under her nose the whole time as she murdered and cursed the other elves.

"Perhaps it wasn't visible until Tinsel decided to reveal it. Perhaps you were the only one who could find it." Hades picked up the box that held the Everbloom and turned it in his hands. "He was powerful and clever enough to steal it from the queen and to evade her for seven decades. I'll bet even after his death, even after he was cursed, he managed to hold on to enough power to keep it hidden."

I nodded, thinking that Tinsel wasn't quite the helpless elf

I'd believed. I didn't know why he'd stolen the flower, but clearly he'd committed a crime. And he'd embroiled the others in it as well—assuming that they were part of the heist to begin with. But they'd already been punished far more than the crime should have called for. The others were free. I could only hope that Bronwyn's magical, musical, gem-encrusted bird would buy Tinsel's freedom.

"I want to hold off going through the portal until tomorrow," I told Hades. "Just so I can finalize everything and so Cassie and the others can organize their defense of the town."

Just in case everything fell apart. I wanted the town to be ready. I wanted to be ready, to tie up loose ends since there was a chance I might not be returning. My biggest worry was Maude. I needed to make one more attempt to resurrect her before I left. If it didn't work, then I was going to tell her it wasn't possible. I'd have Nash to arrange for a reaper to escort her back to heaven. But in order for a reaper to do that, I'd need those angels Hades had been dealing with.

Which meant I had to tell him. This might be the last night I ever saw him. I loved his gentlemanly approach, but I was hoping we could fast-track this relationship a bit since it might be the most short-lived romance I ever had.

"Things might be different in their world," Hades warned me. "A lot of things might be different there."

True. And from what I'd learned about the various fae-lands, they were a mess of convoluted hidden meanings. One wrong word and someone could lose their freedom, or their firstborn child. But this crime hadn't happened in their world, it had happened here, and that pissed me off.

"They entered our lands, our town, and killed an entire settlement of elves." My blood boiled as I mentally rehashed the slaughter that had taken place right under our noses—a slaughter we'd been unaware of for decades. It was humiliating. Their queen, or whatever assassin they'd sent, had no right to do that. They'd committed a crime in *our* town, on *our* watch, against beings *we* were duty bound to protect. I wanted to do something about it. I wanted Cassie to do something about it. She was the head witch. She was in charge. Yes, the elves had been murdered when we'd all still been children, but it was our duty to set things right, to see justice done.

The dead elves wanted justice, and I couldn't let them down. Cassie and my sisters might be able to live with the painful knowledge that a crime had gone unpunished, but I couldn't. I'd hear their voices, see their faces every night. The dead belonged to me, just as the living belonged to Cassie. I couldn't deny them their justice.

Besides, Savior Mountain was the only acceptable spot for Clinton's pack. They'd already drilled wells, put up solar panels, and built houses. They couldn't move, and there was no way the pack could continue to live on a haunted mountain. It wasn't just the dead elves that needed help, it was the werewolves as well.

And as we'd all learned, unhappy werewolves made for an unhappy Accident.

I looked up at Hades. "I'll trade the Everbloom for the town's safety, give Bronwyn's gift in return for Tinsel's freedom. Then I'll come home."

"But you might not come back." Hades held out his hands. "You've lived with fae your whole life. You know how they are. The queen will take the Everbloom from you because she considers it hers, and she'll take the gift as well. Then she'll find some loophole that means she can keep you in her kingdom forever."

Cassie wouldn't let that happen. Neither would any of my sisters or their mates. But it would still take forever for them to figure out how to reach me in the elven lands and in the end I still might never be free.

"I have to do this." I rubbed my face, trying to think of some way this might work. "There's no other choice, and I've made a deal. Fae take these bargains seriously. There's no going back on a deal. If I don't show up, then she'll consider it an act of war."

Hades took my hand, entwining his fingers in mine. "I...I know of a way to keep you safe, to prevent the elf queen from holding you hostage. You'll be able to return home. Well, not home actually, but somewhere safe. And then I can bring you home from there. But you'd need to trust me, and to trust me, I need to tell you something first."

I caught my breath. He had a way out? My biggest fear hadn't been that the elf queen would kill me. From what I knew of fae courtesy, murdering me was out of the question. We had negotiated a contract. I was bringing her the item she requested and a gift. I would be considered a guest in her kingdom. But there was nothing in their convoluted societal rules to keep her from refusing to let me leave and imprisoning me forever.

I did trust Hades. And I was absolutely on board for whatever he was about to propose.

"Go on," I urged him.

He took a deep breath. "I was married once. Before."

My eyes widened, then I felt a fool for being so shocked. I'd read the myths and legends, and while they often got things wrong, there was usually a good bit of truth in them.

"Persephone?" I asked.

He nodded. "It was a long time ago. We were both young. And looking back, it was a terrible match. But I was so in love and I tried to do anything I could to make her stay. Anything. In spite of that, she was never happy. She wanted to live half the year apart and half with me, and I agreed. We did that for centuries. I was miserable when she was away. She was miserable when we were together—which meant I was basically miserable all the time. One year she never returned, and I found our bonding token on my doorstep. No word. No explanation. Nothing."

"Oh, Hades." My fingers gripped his. "I'm so sorry."

I knew what it was like to love someone, only to have them ghost you. The lack of resolution was crippling. I'd spent months thinking Cameron might come back, wondering if I'd done something wrong. I hated that Hades had gone through the same thing.

He smiled at me. "I'm okay now. I mean, I don't love her anymore, and like I said, looking back I realize how horribly wrong that relationship was. She needed a constant stream of new and exciting, and I'm very content with my routine and familiar comforts. We were a terrible match."

I nodded, still thinking of Cameron. He'd been the same way. And looking back, we'd been a terrible match as well. He'd done me a favor by leaving that day, I just wished he hadn't done it in such a dickhead way.

Hades let out a breath and smiled sadly. "But I'd be lying if I said the whole thing left me unscathed. I have been reluctant to risk my heart again. I've thrown myself into my work. When I met you, it was like a lightning bolt struck me and lit me up from inside. Every moment I spend with you, I admire and care about you even more. I felt the stirrings of love for you there in that bar, and they have grown in the days since. But I need to proceed slowly. I'm afraid that I might make a mistake again—a mistake my heart may not recover from this time."

I squeezed his hand. "I feel the same about you. And I've had a relationship end much like your marriage did. It leaves scars."

His smile warmed. "We're both equally scarred. And

while I'm sad that you were hurt as I was, I know that a shared experience means we can truly understand each other's feelings and fears."

I let go of his hand and clasped my fingers together, trying to work up the nerve to confess my own secret, but he continued.

"I'm a bit embarrassed to admit this, but when Persephone and I married, part of the ceremony included something where I could always call her to my side." He shifted, looking down. "I didn't trust that she'd come home to me. That was a huge red-flag, as the humans would say. I should have known then that the marriage was doomed, but we went on with the ceremony. In addition to our marriage token, she ate an enchanted fruit which was spelled to always bring her to my side if I called her."

Hades took a round and red fruit out of his pocket and put it on the table.

I stared at the pomegranate, then at his pants. "Did you have that in your pocket the whole time? Do you normally walk around with fruit in your pants pockets?"

And how the hell did that thing actually fit in his pocket anyway? I liked to think I would have noticed if Hades had a huge round bulge that was to the left of where I'd expect to be seeing a huge round bulge.

What else was he carrying in his pants? A pineapple? A tennis racket? A 1990 Geo Metro?

"It's a magical item," he explained. "I called it to me. I don't carry it around in my pocket all the time. It's not like I ever expected to use it again. Ever. The first time…that was disastrous. It showed a lack of trust on my part, and I'm mortified to even be confessing this to you. The only reason I'm telling you about it is because I think in this case, the fruit might actually be used for something good."

I suddenly realized where he was going with this, and I

felt my face heat up—just as embarrassed as he was at the idea. We were nowhere near this point in our relationship. Not at all. We hadn't even kissed yet, let alone be at the marriage-token, pomegranate-eating stage.

He pushed the fruit over to me. "If you accept my marriage token and eat the fruit, then no matter where you are, I can always call you to my side. The elf queen can never keep you against your will. No one can."

I picked up the fruit in suddenly sweaty hands, surprised by how heavy it was. The thought of taking this step terrified me.

"You eat it." Hades squirmed, his gaze everywhere but on me. "After you've taken my token. We'll be married."

I barely knew him. Daydreams of me and Hades living in his beautiful afterlife were one thing, but the reality of that sort of commitment was something I was so not ready for.

"You sure I can't just take the fruit with me into the elf lands and throw it at the queen if she gets out of line? I'll bet it could do some serious damage as a projectile weapon."

He stared at me blankly, my lame attempt at a joke clearly falling flat.

"You could wait to eat it until you're at the elf-queen's court, but I worry that it may be taken from you before you have the chance. Best to do it beforehand. Besides, to work correctly, you'd need to have already accepted my marriage token, waiting to eat the fruit wouldn't allow you to evade the wedding portion of the spell."

This clearly wasn't a time for humor, and I knew Hades was risking his pride to even suggest such a thing, but I was scared. And I had questions.

"So I'm assuming if I accept your marriage token and eat this, I'll be living at your place September to March for all of eternity?"

Hades actually blushed. "If you want. I mean, you can

always just leave the marriage token on my doorstep and break the spell."

Like Persephone had done. This was such a mess. It was a perfect way to ensure I'd have an out if the elf queen tried to kidnap me, but in the end I'd either be married to someone I really didn't know well enough to take that step with, or repeat the action that had previously broken his heart and basically annul the whole thing.

Could we move forward afterward? Would this whole pomegranate thing keep me safe, but wind up being the very thing that destroyed a relationship with someone who could possibly be the love of my life?

I turned the pomegranate over in my hands. "Did you have kids together? You and Persephone?"

"No. She wanted children. I did too, but somehow I must have known our marriage wouldn't last because I told her I wanted to wait."

Sheesh, we hadn't even kissed and here we were talking about marriage and children. I wasn't even sure how I felt about having kids, let alone whether or not I wanted to have them with Hades. I liked children. I got the impression Hades would be an amazing father. And I wanted to do all the things my mother hadn't done—I wanted to raise my kids like Cassie had raised me.

If I had them, that is.

I set the pomegranate back down on the table. "Let's go over the steps here. Tell me how the fruit-wedding token combo works."

"We say our vows and exchange tokens. In the human tradition, it's rings, so I assume that's what you'd want." He eyed me worriedly. "Then you eat the pomegranate—"

"The whole thing?" I wrinkled my nose, thinking the rind, or shell, or whatever the hell it was called was going to be kinda difficult to choke down.

"Just the seeds. So you eat it, and we're linked. Married, actually. But it doesn't have to be forever. When you get back from dealing with the elf queen, just put my token on my doorstep—"

"Is there a better, less insulting way to annul our marriage?" I asked. "I'm not going to just dump the ring on your doorstep and walk away. I mean, first I don't even know where your doorstep is or how to get there. Secondly, that's rude as shit. I like you. I want to explore this thing with you and see if it turns into love, into something permanent. I might end up wanting that ring back one day, and ending our temporary marriage the same way your ex-wife left you doesn't feel like something that would lead to a possible future together."

His whole body relaxed and he blew out a breath. I knew this had been hard for him, but I hadn't realized that he was just as terrified of this whole thing as I was.

"I don't want it to feel like I'm rejecting you," I said softly. "I just want to be able to take about a hundred steps back in our relationship, so we can take our time getting there. So we're sure. So we enjoy the romance and the journey. I appreciate you offering to do this for me. If I say yes to the fruit and the marriage, I don't want it to dredge up any more bad memories and parallels with your ex-wife than absolutely necessary."

He smiled. "I appreciate that. And yes, you can just give the marriage token back to me when you return."

Why hadn't he told me that in the beginning instead of assuming I was just going to toss it at his door and run off? The fact that he'd immediately made that leap let me know that Hades really did carry some baggage about his ex-wife. Which was okay. I had baggage, too. Together we'd work through this. Slowly.

And now that we understood each other's intentions and

fears, it was time to lighten this up a bit.

"I'll have you know my sisters are going to kill me if they find out I got married without them," I teased. "If we ever do this for real, I'm going to need a white dress, and a huge ceremony in Accident—probably catered by Glenda. I'll ask her to make a pomegranate wedding cake."

His gaze met mine, and my heart lurched at the tentative hope in his eyes.

"White might not be the best choice of colors if the wedding ceremony is going to involve the messy eating of a bright red fruit," he commented. "Maybe you should change tradition and be married in black, or wine-red. Or you could always wear a bib for the fruit-eating part of the wedding."

I stared at him a second then burst out laughing. I'd caught a hint of dry humor from him before, but this was downright funny.

"Wedding bibs for everyone," I pronounced. "We'll have Eshu stand at the door and hand them out to all the guests. Unless you plan on having Eshu be your groomsman."

His eyes widened. "Oh, hell no."

I giggled. "Bibs. We'll all eat pomegranates. Maybe have one of those hands-free pie eating contests. Or a food fight."

"My darling, I will gladly sign on for pie-eating or food fights for our real marriage." He tilted his head as he regarded me, his gaze warm. "But we should plan on something more intimate and informal for our temporary, get-out-of-elfland marriage."

Darling. He'd called me darling. The implications of that endearment sent a rush of heat through me. Yes, I was not-so-slowly falling in love with this guy. He was goofy, nerdy, and kind. He was smart, creative, and dependable. He was gorgeous, and I loved every moment I spent with him.

"I can do informal and intimate," I teased. "We say a few words. I eat a fruit. Do we need to consummate this marriage afterward? Please tell me we need to consummate the marriage."

Red surged up Hade's neck clear to the roots of his hair. "It's not necessary. I mean, for the spell to work, we don't have to do that. But we do need to kiss. Is that okay?"

He was so silly. Shy. And adorably awkward. "Yes, it's more than okay."

I was on board with more than kissing, but willing to take this as slow as he wanted. He was risking everything, offering me this. I didn't want to push the envelope too far and take a chance I'd destroy what we'd been building over the last few days.

He looked down again. "When you return, I really want to show you the afterlife I've created—The Underworld. I hope you'll like it, that maybe we can spend some time there. On dates or something. It's my home. Or it will be once I'm done with all these contracts in hell."

"I'd love that." I reached out to touch the pomegranate, thinking that we should probably do this informal, intimate marriage ceremony tonight. Maybe back at my house, where if that kiss led to something more, we'd have a nice comfortable bed nearby.

Shit. I'd completely forgotten about Maude. I hadn't told him about Maude yet. My smile faded, thinking that this whole thing might be blown all to hell once I revealed my secret. Hades had risked everything to tell me his past hurts, and to offer me this out. I couldn't let him marry me—even a temporary marriage—without him knowing what I'd done.

I twisted my fingers together, took a deep breath, and looked up at him. "There's something I need to confess to you before we go any further. And I totally understand if you want to rescind your offer. I understand if you never want to see me ever again. I...I did something really bad. And I lied by omission to you. I know that might be a deal breaker, but I just need to get it all out on the table."

"What is it?"

His voice was so gentle, his gaze so kind that I almost cried.

"I'm...I'm the necromancer who stole that soul from heaven," I blurted out. "I didn't mean to. Addy and I were under attack, and I panicked. I raised zombies from a nearby family cemetery, and when I returned them all to their graves, one didn't go back. She's been living with me ever since, and I've been trying to figure out how to fully resurrect her. She wants a second life, and since this was all my fault, I vowed to do everything I could to make that happen. But clearly I suck as a necromancer, because nothing I do works, and she's this zombie who can't leave my house. But then I met you and found out that her being gone is causing you problems and might end up causing a war between heaven and hell, and I don't know what to do. The angels won't be happy until she's returned, but I made her a promise. It's such a mess, and I understand if you never want to see me ever again."

There. Done. And while it felt very cleansing to tell him, I was miserable, worried about Maude's future. And Hade's and my future—which might now be nothing.

"Hey."

I glanced up at his soft word and blinked away my tears.

"I already knew you were the one," he said. "I've known for a day now. The souls were called to defend the Hoffman farm against demons, and when I interviewed the demons involved, they told me about you and Addy. You were there. Your sister was being attacked. You're a necromancer."

I sucked in a breath. "You knew? And you didn't turn me in? You didn't tell *anyone*? Not even Lucien?"

He reached out and tucked a strand of hair behind my

ear. "Of course I didn't turn you in, Babylon. These past few days have taught me how kind and generous you are. I've seen how you care about those you love as well as those you feel responsible for. We all make mistakes. I admire you for working so hard to correct yours and to help this woman. And I'm honored you trust me enough to tell me your secret."

"You're not mad?" I whispered. "You don't hate me for not telling you right away? Or for doing dark magic?"

He sighed. "Babylon, I built the very structure of hell. Dark is in the eye of the beholder. There is nothing wrong with necromancy. Many are afraid of those who have power over the dead, but I simply see it as yet another magic—one that intrigues me. You did what you needed to do. Your only error was in not having the training or the knowledge to perform the magic you attempted. And that's not your fault. You grew up in a family of witches where no one has ever been gifted with necromantic magic."

"But I didn't tell you," I insisted.

"You'd just met me," he countered. "I'm not foolish enough to expect you'd confide all your secrets to me over French toast within hours of our first meeting. I hadn't told you I'd been married. You didn't tell me you were living with a zombie you'd raised and were trying to resurrect."

He was right. And I realized all the worry I'd had over trusting him had been in vain. Hades was kind, understanding, and I could one hundred percent trust him.

I loved him. And I hoped when this was all over, that eventually I would wear his ring for real.

"What are we going to do about Maude?" I asked. We. Because I knew he'd help me with this just as he was helping me with everything else I was facing.

He stood, then came around to take my hand as I rose from my chair. "Well, I think the first thing we should do is go to your house so I can meet this Maude. Then the three of us can discuss possible courses of action. I feel she should be a part of this discussion, given that she is more than the usual zombie and that you've made her promises."

He was right. I stepped in to brush my lips against his cheek, then smiled up at him.

"An excellent plan, as always. Come on. I want to show you my home. And introduce you to my roommate."

# CHAPTER 22

## BABYLON

*J* could tell that Maude wasn't quite what Hades had been expecting, but he hid his dismay well, and was charming and polite as I made the introductions.

Maude was ecstatic. I'd never seen her so happy or animated. She rushed off to the kitchen to grab food and drink from the fridge, telling him that she wished she were in better condition to cook. With cheese and crackers and some wine, we all sat down in the living room. Maude showed Hades her crochet project, and I sat back with my wine, bemused to see Hades sitting next to a zombie, admiring her half-finished blanket.

"So I hear you want to live a second life," Hades said to her once he'd complimented her handiwork.

She glanced over at me, and I nodded for her to be honest.

"Yes, I do. But I know it may not be possible. Babylon has tried, and time may be running out. She's said that my disappearance has been noticed, and someone may come for me. If that happens, then I won't have a choice but to go with them—I won't risk Babylon's safety by trying to stay. And I'm starting to get tired of existing in this decaying body. I don't want to be like this for years, and it's not fair to have Babylon keep trying over and over, spending so much time on trying to resurrect me."

"I don't mind," I reassured her. But I knew she was right. Time was running out. And I knew it was hard for her living as a zombie, trapped inside my house and unable to leave, or to truly live.

"I'll keep your presence here a secret either until Babylon is successful, or until you decide you'd like to go back to heaven," Hades told her. "I'll buy you as much time as you need."

Maude patted him on the arm. "I appreciate it, but please don't risk yourself or your reputation because of me. If things get dire, or it looks like the angels might attack hell over this, then I'll go back. I don't want anyone hurt because I selfishly want a second chance at life."

We chatted for a while, then Maude went into her bedroom, not so subtly giving us privacy.

"What do you think?" I asked Hades once her door was shut.

He glanced over at Maude's room. "I think she's a lovely, charming woman. I absolutely understand why you're trying to help her out, and I'll support you any way you need."

"But…" I added.

He sighed. "But I worry that she'll be discovered. She's safe here, but the angels are insistent, and there are enough people who know what went down that night you brought her from the grave, that a few clues may have slipped out— enough that someone will add them up and you'll end up with a reaper at your door accompanied by either an angel or a demon."

I nodded, depressed to realize he was right. "The spell I found seems to work a little, but for some reason I just can't manage to fully resurrect her. Maybe I just don't have enough power."

"You'll gain power as you grow older," Hades said. "But Maude doesn't have the time to wait for that."

"Nor does she want to wait that long." I frowned, an idea forming in my mind. "I'm wondering…"

He shifted on the couch to face me. "What?"

"My sisters all grew in power when they fell in love. There's something about the pairing of a demon and a witch that amps up the levels of both partners."

"I'm not a demon," he reminded me.

I noticed that he didn't mention anything about love. Truth was, I was more than halfway in love with him, and from what he'd said earlier, I knew he felt the same. Maybe that wouldn't be enough, but it was worth a try.

"Neither is Eshu, but Sylvie got a power boost when they got together. Same with Ophelia and Nash. He's a reaper, and not technically a demon either."

"I'm willing to give it a try." He reached out and touched my arm. "I just don't want you to be disappointed if I do nothing for you."

Oh, he did everything for me. I scooted closer to him—so close our shoulders touched. "Maybe we should get married first. The vows might help."

He nodded, then shifted on the sofa so he could reach in his pants pocket. First he pulled out a pair of plain gold bands that hummed with power.

"These are not the same tokens as my first marriage," he reassured as he passed the larger ring to me.

I didn't bother asking why he was carrying around a brand new set of wedding rings. Maybe he'd just magicked them up out of nowhere seconds ago. Hades dug in his pocket again, this time pulling out the pomegranate.

He set the fruit on the coffee table in front of us, then took my hands in his.

"Babylon Perkins, witch of Accident, you are the one I love and cherish most among the living and the dead. I am yours. I will always be yours until you wish otherwise. As I place this ring upon your finger, I give you a sliver of myself to carry with you always so that you know my thoughts, my heart, my very soul are in your hands."

Tears pricked the back of my eyes at his vow. As he slid the band on my left-hand ring finger I felt a wave of warmth roll through me, lighting me up from inside.

"Hades, architect of The Underworld, creator of afterlife, you are first in my thoughts and in my heart. I vow to walk with you in this life and in the next, to be your partner in all things. I promise to always be honest with you, to honor you, to treat you with loving kindness. With this ring, I give you a piece of myself, so that I am always by your side."

I slid the ring on his finger and he curled his hands around mind. Our eyes met, and he leaned forward to kiss me.

It was a soft gentle kiss, but so full of promise. His lips brushed mine, lingering for a brief second for us to share a breath. As he started to pull back, he stopped then kissed me again, this one with barely restrained passion.

We broke apart, still holding hands.

"I want to take you into your bedroom and do far more than just kiss you," he said, his voice husky. "But I don't want to rush things between us. Rushing in the past has always led to heartbreak and disaster."

I nodded. "For me, too. I'll wait—although it won't be easy. Hopefully taking it slow means a few days? Weeks? A month? Because I don't think I can wait for years."

He laughed. "Me either. We'll move forward at our own pace. If that's a day or two weeks or a month, then I'm okay with that. I'm going to admit I'm hoping it's a day. Maybe a week at most."

I wanted him now, but I knew making love with Hades would be even better if I let our love grow first. Hopefully our love grew fast.

"Time to eat the pomegranate." He picked up the fruit and handed it to me. "These seeds strengthen our bond. As you eat them, we will be as one. Inseparable until the bond is broken by one of us. No being among the living or the dead can ever keep us from each other. Forever we will be joined."

I picked up a decorative athame from a display on my coffee table and carefully cut the fruit in half. Red juice ran down my fingers and hands, dripping onto my pants. Scooping the seeds out of the pomegranate, I ate them. By the time I'd finished half the fruit, I had juice staining my mouth and chin, my hands, my shirt and my pants. I was a sticky mess, and didn't care one bit about it.

"Forever we will be joined," I told Hades as I handed him the other half of the fruit.

It might not be traditional, but what was good for the goose was good for the gander.

"Now I can summon you to my side whenever I want as well," I teased as he ate the seeds.

He smiled, his shirt and hands equally covered in red juice. "I don't know if it works that way. I hope so. It would be nice if anytime you needed me, you could call and I would arrive. I'd like that."

It was sad that Persephone had never thought to do this in their ceremony. Had she not cared about wanting to call Hades to her? Had she seen this as a shackle, as a lack of trust, rather than the symbol of partnership and oneness that I saw?

Hades chuckled and held out the pomegranate rind, looking down at his sticky, stained hands. "We are a mess. Do you have a wet towel in the kitchen? If we knew each other for longer than a few days, I'd suggest a shower together, but I think a towel will have to do."

Why did he have to mention showering together? Now I was stirred up, thinking of the two of us naked with hot water hitting our skin. Soaping each other up. Making love as the spray beat down upon us.

Towel. Wet towel.

"Yes." I jumped up, flustered. "In the kitchen."

He followed me in. We threw away the empty pomegranate rinds. Then we washed our hands and dried them. I held out my red-splotched shirt, thinking I should change.

"Leave it." He leaned in and kissed me again. "I like seeing the stains on your shirt and pants."

Suddenly this sticky mess was sexy. As were the rings on our fingers.

"Wait. I almost forgot something." Hades took my hand and waved his over the ring. "Now they're invisible to everyone but us."

It was a good idea. My sisters would definitely spot the rings tomorrow, and there would be questions. Better to keep this whole thing secret for now. Plus I liked the idea of having this just between the two of us. It felt special and intimate that we were the only ones who could see the rings.

"Do you want to try to resurrect Maude again tonight?" he asked. "Or maybe wait until you get back."

"I want to do it now." I was still worried that somehow I wouldn't make it back from the elven lands. It was the right thing to try one more time before I left, just in case I didn't return.

Hades nodded. "I'll go get her. You gather whatever supplies you need and I'll meet you in the living room. Unless you want to do it somewhere else?"

"It's a small house. I tend to do most of my magic at the

dining room table." I chuckled. "Much to Maude's dismay. Even covering the table, she always pitches a fit. Seems that it's not sanitary to perform magic the same place you sit down for dinner."

He wrinkled his nose. "I agree with Maude on this one."

"It's the only spot that's large enough," I argued.

"Maybe the dining room table is for magic, and dinner can be somewhere else." He shot me a shy smile. "Or maybe you can just always have dinner out. With me."

"If you're paying, I'll go for that."

I bent down to pull the candles from the kitchen cabinet then took them into the dining room. I had studied this spell enough that by the time Hades and Maude walked into the room, I had the table covered, the candles arranged, and the spices and incense ready to go.

"You, stand behind me here," I instructed Hades as Maude took her place in front of me. It was dark out, and with the heavy curtains, I didn't need to lower the blackout shades as before. I shut off the lights, then lit the candles, knowing where everything was by memory.

"Babylon?" Maude whispered. "I don't...I know I need to be naked, and that was fine when it was just you and me, but..."

I'd been focused on the ritual and not thought about how Maude would feel being nude in front of Hades. I needed him to help me power the spell, but I understood her discomfort.

"I'll close my eyes," Hades offered. "And if I need to open them to do something, I'll be sure to keep my gaze lowered and away from you."

Maude waited as he shut his eyes and had turned slightly so he wasn't facing her. Then she disrobed.

Her skin was in much better shape than it had been when I first pulled her from the grave. The previous spell had done a lot to restore her hair as well. But she still definitely looked dead. Hoping this time the spell would work, I got busy lighting the myrrh incense, then rubbing her all over with the cedar oil.

That done I stood in front of her, holding the spices and other oils.

"Refresh." I placed a dot of tea tree oil on Maude's forehead.

"Renew." I placed a dot of peppermint oil over her heart.

"Restore." I bent down to brush rose oil over the tops of her feet, then stood.

"Revive." Picking up the sprigs of thyme, I brushed them over her lips, then in a vertical line down her body.

"Rebirth." I repeated the process with sprigs of lavender. That done, I set everything aside and picked up the last bit of the cinnamon candy Bronwyn had spelled for me.

"Are you ready?" I asked Maude.

She nodded and opened her mouth.

"Resurrect." I placed the candy between her lips and she closed her mouth around it. Stepping back, I put a hand on Hades's chest. "Put your arms around me and hold me close."

I felt him do as I asked. His arms were strong around my waist, his body warm against my back. I could feel his breath stirring my hair and I smiled, just happy to have him here, to be so close to him.

But this ritual wasn't about us, it was about Maude.

"Maude Hoffman, you have been called from the grave to live a second life," I pronounced. "Live once more, body and soul. A new day. A new life."

I felt the magic pour from me. The flames of the candles flickered. The scent of myrrh filled my nose. Then my aura changed. Another's joined in, deepening and enriching the spell. The burgundy of my magic was suddenly infused with black and gold, making it rich, complex, and breathtakingly powerful.

For a second nothing happened, then Maude glowed with a white light that grew until I had to close my eyes against its brightness. Suddenly the world went dark, and I opened my eyes to find the light gone, the candles gutted, and the incense no longer burning.

"Maude?"

"I'm...I'm okay. I think."

Her voice had lost that raspy, breathy quality. I stepped out of Hade's arms and felt my way along the wall for the light switch, hardly daring to hope. Flicking the switch, I turned and gasped.

Maude stood before me, alive and well. But she hadn't been resurrected into the elderly woman she'd been at her death. No, the Maude before me looked to be my age with reddish blonde hair, and smooth pale skin dotted with freckles. Her eyes weren't that milky blue, but a whisky-brown. She smiled, parting full lips along a wide mouth.

The spell had worked. It had worked better than I'd ever expected.

Picking up a mirror I used for spells, I handed it to her. She'd been inspecting her hands and body, but she took the glass, looked in it and began to cry.

"Oh Babylon! You did it. You and Hades did it. I'll never be able to repay you for this gift you've given me. Thank you. Thank you so much."

She put the mirror down and hugged me. Maude had her second life. I could cross into the elven lands tomorrow without worrying about this unfinished business. There were still the angels to contend with, but Maude had her second life. She could meet Rita and the rest of her family. She could walk out in the sun, get a job, eat food. She could bake that peach crumble that she'd been so famous for, and actually get to enjoy it once more.

I'd righted my wrong. There might be some loose ends to clean up, but I'd righted my wrong. And I couldn't have done any of this without Hades.

"Um, ladies?" Hades asked. "Is Maude dressed yet? Because I'd really like to see what all the excitement is about."

Oh no! I laughed, realizing that we'd completely forgotten about his promise to keep his eyes closed. Maude grabbed her dress off the floor, but I stilled her hand.

"No. There's no need for you to ever wear that again. Go into my room, *Ann*, and get something of mine out of the closet to wear until you can go shopping."

Ann. Her chosen name for her second life. She did a little dance, delighted that I'd remembered, and skipped off to my room.

I waited for her to leave, then smiled over at my husband —my *husband*! Walking over, I stood in front of him.

"I love you," I told him. His eyes flew open, and I kissed him, showing exactly how I felt about him right now and always.

# CHAPTER 23

## BABYLON

*I* spent the night curled up in Hades's arms, just being near each other. The next morning I gave Ann some money and told her to go shopping for clothes, food, books, and anything else she might need as she began to live her second life. As Hades and I drove out to Savior Mountain, I thought about the woman. It would probably be best if she stayed in my house for at least a few weeks getting used to life again. I'd help her find a job, start looking for an apartment, introduce her around as a distant cousin from out of state or something.

I'd definitely introduce her to Rita, but I wasn't sure about what to do with the rest of her family. Maude had a living daughter and several grandchildren who might pick up that Ann looked exactly like their long lost relative.

Hades reached out and took my hand. "A penny for your thoughts?"

"Cheapskate," I teased.

"Then a million dollars for your thoughts?"

I laughed. "*That's* a little extreme. I was just thinking of Ann and how to get her situated. How to get her a job. How to introduce her to her former family. I'll give you the million back if you tell me your thoughts."

"On Ann as well. Only I'm trying to figure out how I'm going to tell the angels what happened."

I grimaced. "Will they demand I suffer some sort of punishment for what I've done? I stole one of their souls and resurrected it. I doubt they're going to be okay with that whole thing."

"No, they won't. The good thing is that people are always doing things that anger heaven, and history is filled with necromancers who do, or try to do, exactly what you've done. The punishment is that you won't be allowed in heaven."

I sighed. "I doubt I was heading there anyway as a witch and a necromancer. Besides, from what you've described, I'm not sure I'd like it anyway."

"What I won't tell them is that you're not going to some circle of hell to swim in lava and be poked with a pitchfork. You're coming to The Underworld." He shot me a quick glance. "If you want to, that is. I mean, you don't have to come to my afterlife. And you've got a lifetime to decide."

I hid a smile. "Are there lava pits in The Underworld? Will you chase me around with a pitchfork?"

He chuckled. "If that's what you want, then yes I will chase you around with a pitchfork in my hand. I'll even poke you with it, if you like. No lava pits, though. After spending all this time in hell, I'm sick of lava pits. I tried to get them to be more inventive, to think of other punishments, but no. Every circle has lava pits. And hot coals. And pitchforks."

"And Cliffs of Despair?" I asked.

He puffed out his chest. "There is only one Cliffs of Despair. I refused to budge on that. And it was completely my design. The redesign is going to be phenomenal as well."

My lips twitched. "I'm sure it will be."

We fell silent as I pulled into the werewolf compound. The wolves were grouped over by the alpha's house, while everyone else was at the lumberyard. Hades and I got out and walked, hand-in-hand, to where Cassie stood, poking a finger at the shimmer of air that surrounded the portal.

"What *is* this?" she asked, poking it once more.

"I created a temporary pocket dimension to hold the portal," Hades explained. "Just in case the queen sent more darts through it, or decided to attack. No one and nothing gets in or out until I bring the portal back."

"So it's not really here?" Cassie circled the encased portal. "I can see it, but it's not here."

"It's like a window." Hades wrinkled his nose and thought for a second. "Like when you Facetime someone on your cell phone. You can see them, but they're not in the room with you."

"That has got to be the most amazing bit of magic I've ever seen." She sent Hades an admiring glance. "I like you. You can marry Babylon. I'm giving that union my approval."

I choked a bit at her mention of marriage, glancing down at the rings that Hades had assured me only we could see.

"Thank you for your blessing of our future union." Hades winked at me. "Are we prepared? Should I bring the portal back?"

"Here's the gift for the queen." Bronwyn stepped forward and handed me the beautiful enchanted bird.

"And I have the Everbloom." I put the bird safely in my bag that held the box with the elven artifact.

"We're ready to defend Accident if the queen attacks." Cassie motioned toward my sisters and their demon mates, all of them encircling the portal. "The werewolves are our second line of defense, and I've warned the residents in town to be prepared, just in case."

I took a deep breath and let it out before nodding at Hades. "Then I'm ready."

He snapped his fingers and the shimmering air became just regular air. The portal expanded slightly, as if sensing I was about to enter. I took a step forward, but Hades halted me.

"Just one more thing." He leaned in and kissed me. I was pretty sure my sisters, their boyfriends, and all the were-wolves were hooting and whistling, but all I knew at that moment was Hades.

"By my side, always," he whispered as his lips left mine.

"By my side, always," I replied slightly louder, so that my family and the others could hear. No matter what happened, I wanted them to know that Hades was important to me—just as important as their mates were to them.

"I will see you soon." Hades kissed me once more, then I stepped through the portal and into the elven lands.

The portal put me into a large chamber that reminded me of the church that Rita and Ralph had been married in. At the end opposite me, down a long grassy walkway, stood a dais. At the very top, on an ornate throne, sat the elf queen. There were three elves on either side of her, and both sides of the walkway to the dais were lined with crowds of elves.

They all had colorful hair, and huge eyes that sparkled like faceted gems. They wore silk robes, and all of them had long hair that was styled to reveal the pointed tips of their ears. Beams of colored light danced around the chamber, highlighting the trees, flowers, and grass that grew inside this strange place.

It was beautiful. They were beautiful. But with my first step along the grassy pathway, I knew something was wrong. Something about the place just felt off, and it wasn't because I was unfamiliar with elf customs or worlds other than the one I inhabited. No, the place felt as if it were decaying, as if some renewing force was missing.

It was then that I realized Tinsel had lied. The Everbloom wasn't some pretty bauble prized by the queen that she might not miss for a century or so if it went missing, it was the lifeblood of their land. Tinsel had stolen the very essence of this place and escaped with his friends to create a new land somewhere else, and in doing so, he'd sent his homeland and all the other elves into decline. His friends had to have known what he'd done.

How many centuries or millennium would it take before this place and the elves all died? I knew now why the queen was so harsh in her punishment—and why, in spite of her casual attitude toward the Everbloom, she was so desperate to have it back. Tinsel had been a traitor in her eyes, and probably in the eyes of the other elves here. I had no idea what events had led up to him stealing the Everbloom. I didn't know enough about the situation to place blame. But I did know that the Everbloom needed to be returned, regardless of what had happened before.

"Do you have it?" The queen's voice didn't quite hide that note of desperation I'd overlooked before.

"Yes. I have the Everbloom."

Voices erupted in exclamation and comment, but the queen didn't quiet them. I passed by the gathered crowds, climbing the steps until I stood before her. With a respectful bow, I took the box from my bag and opened it. Taking the tiny glass orchid out of the box, I placed it by her feet and stepped down from the dais.

The Everbloom shook, then cracked in half. I had a second of panic, thinking that maybe I'd somehow broken it, then tendrils shot out from the pieces of glass. Vines crawled across the floor, climbed the walls, covered the ceiling overhead. Even with the thick canopy, the rays of colored lights shone through. Suddenly the vines burst into bloom and the crowd collectively gasped.

The lights were brighter. The elves glowed. The whole chamber appeared sharp and clear, as if I'd been wearing thick grime-covered glasses and removed them. I *felt* the difference. Within seconds, the Everbloom had renewed every living thing, every structure, every blade of grass. It reminded me of when Maude had been resurrected.

The love of the living and the dead. Renewal. Rebirth. Resurrection. Maybe it hadn't been coincidence that the cursed tree had come down across the road to the werewolf compound, and that Clinton had come to me. Maybe it wasn't a coincidence that I was the one to find the Everbloom. Maybe it wasn't a coincidence that I'd taken credit for Sylvie's spell and bargained with the elf queen. The Everbloom bridged life and death. I bridged life and death. I was proud that I was the one to bring it home and bring renewal to these elves.

But there was one more item on my agenda for today. Tinsel may have been wrong to steal the Everbloom, but I'd vowed to free him, and I felt he'd suffered more than enough as his punishment.

"We agreed that if the Everbloom was brought back, that we would not attack you or your people or your town," the queen said. "I will uphold that bargain."

"We have a second bargain, your highness." I reached into my bag and took out Bronwyn's gift. "I have something to present to you, and we agreed that if this gift pleases you and you decide to accept it, you will consider Tinsel's punishment to be over and free him from his curse, allowing his soul to journey to his afterlife."

The crowd murmured, some clearly not pleased with this bargain, but the queen nodded. "I did make that bargain.

Present your gift, and I will judge if it is worthy of a thief's freedom or not."

With somewhat sweaty hands I carried the little enameled and bejeweled bird up the dais and bent my head as I held it out for the queen.

She took it and turned the item over in her hand as I stepped back down.

"This is beautiful. The artistry is excellent. But as lovely as this is, it is not impressive enough of a gift to secure the release of the thief."

My heart plummeted, and my thoughts raced, trying to think of some other thing I could offer to maybe sweeten the deal.

The queen ran a finger over the jewel-encrusted head of the bird, then tossed it to me. My hands shot up to catch it before it hit the ground and suffered any damage, but before it reached me, the enchanted bird spread its wings and flew. After circling around the chamber, it came to rest on the top of the queen's throne, opened its enameled beak, and sang.

I didn't recognize the song or know any of the words, but as the music poured from the bird's throat, the elves all began to cry. It took me a few seconds before I realized that they were crying tears of joy. Bronwyn had not just enchanted the bird to sing, she'd magicked it to know exactly the song its owner wanted to hear, and to deliver it with perfection.

When the bird finished, even the queen was wiping away a tear. She gazed up and held out her hand. The bird flew from the throne to land on her arm, tilting its head and chirping merrily up at her.

She smiled, and I realized it was the first time I'd ever seen that expression on her face.

"I've changed my mind. I must keep this gift, so that means I also must set the thief free." She looked down at me, her gaze going to the fingers of my left hand. "And as I see you've made some precautions against attempts to keep you here, I will agree to let you return without any hinderance from me or my people. Go. And know that I consider this business between us to be finished."

I backed away, bowing and muttering my thanks. Then I turned and walked as quickly as I dared to the portal, stepping through to the other side. Running past my sisters and the others who were expressing relief and asking questions, I went straight to the log, grabbed my athame and plunged it into the rotted wood. No blood pooled around it. No spirit screamed in agony.

"Tinsel?" I reached out for him and found...nothing.

"The curse is gone," Sylvie said.

"It's just a log," Hades added. "There's nothing magic about it at all. Not even a trace of residual magic."

He was gone. The curse was gone, and Tinsel had been set free. I cast around with my awareness, searching for any sign that he was okay, and a little irritated that he hadn't even stuck around to thank me for freeing him. Maybe he'd been worried that I'd be upset at what he'd done. Maybe he'd been so relieved to be free after all these decades that he'd just taken off. Either way he was gone, and my job here was done. We'd freed him and the others, and broken the curse. Now the werewolves could continue to live here. Accident wouldn't be attacked by the elves. The Everbloom was back where it belonged.

And Maude—or Ann—was beginning a new life.

I couldn't have done it alone. I couldn't have done any of it alone. I'd needed my sisters' help, the fairies, the werewolves, and even the badger shifter. And most of all I'd needed Hades.

Turning, I launched myself into his arms. "I didn't need to use your get-out-of-jail-free card after all."

"I'm a little sad I didn't get to show you The Underworld," he told me as he held me tight.

"I still want to see it. I want a tour."

I pulled away and he took my hand in his, rubbing the gold band on my finger. "You can give this back if you want."

I laughed. "I think I'll keep it just a little while longer. I like knowing I can summon you to my side any time I need and that you can do the same."

"Anytime I need?" He grinned.

"Absolutely." I gave him a quick kiss.

As we parted I noticed Cassie scowling as she watched us. "Keep what just a little while longer? And what's this about summoning each other to your sides?"

"Something to do with fruit." I laughed, so happy, and so much in love. "I'll tell you later. Maybe in a few weeks, maybe in a few months. When we're ready."

"When we're ready," Hades repeated, then he kissed me again, and all the rest of the world just faded away.

# CHAPTER 24

"*T*hat is unacceptable!" Remiel slammed his fist down on the table, causing all of our coffee cups to jump and the wait staff at the Bob Evans to eye him in alarm.

I shrugged. "I know, but what can we do? Necromancers gonna necromance."

"Resurrected." The angel snarled. "No necromancer has been able to pull that off in nearly a thousand years. Who is this necromancer? Who is he? And who helped him? Someone from hell must have helped him pull this off."

"Why would a demon help resurrect an old woman?" Eshu asked, both of us carefully avoiding Remiel's previous question. "It's not like it does us any good having her alive."

"You're hoping to get another shot at her," Zariel insisted. "To convince her to sin so you can enjoy that peach crumble in hell."

"Wouldn't it be easier for a demon to just steal the recipe?" I asked. "Or to get it from one of her living relatives? They've got the recipe, you know, and I doubt they're *all* going to heaven."

"He's got a point," Waffle chimed in.

Cruciel nodded. "There's no sense in making a big fuss about it, Remiel. They found the lost soul, and she's beyond any of our reach now. You'll just have to wait until she dies again. I think even you can manage to hold off for fifty or so years before you get another bite of that peach crumble."

"Or go ask her for some," Eshu added. "I'm sure if you came down her chimney in the middle of the night, she'd let you have some. Maybe even give you a glass of milk to go with it."

"That's Santa Claus," I reminded Eshu.

"Fine," Remiel snapped. "But that necromancer needs to be punished. Someone needs to punish him."

Eshu made that boom-chicka-wow-wow noise and I elbowed him. "The demons have an extensive torture plan in place for necromancers, I assure you. I designed those areas of hell myself, and promise you they are suitably terrifying."

The angels nodded, somewhat mollified. What they didn't know was there was no way Babylon would ever be tortured, or that she would probably not set foot in hell after her death unless it was to visit her sisters.

Always by my side. As long as she wanted to walk with me, in life or in death, I would always welcome her by my side. And I was already at work on some enhancements to my Underworld, that I hoped she'd like.

"Why did this necromancer decide to resurrect Maude Hoffman, and not the others." Waffle frowned. "Do we need to worry about other souls being resurrected? Should we expect the other six Hoffman souls who briefly went missing from hell and the two from Purgatory to vanish one-by-one?"

"I think the necromancer wanted the peach crumble recipe, just like everyone else," I lied. "Clearly out of the souls who were taken from heaven, hell, and purgatory, hers was the only one that knew the recipe. The necromancer probably traded her a second life for that peach crumble."

Remiel nodded, as if this made absolute sense to him. "The other Hoffman souls are not particularly gifted in cooking, so I assume they're safe."

"Yeah," Zariel grumbled. "I wish they were gifted in cooking."

"So are we done here?" Waffle looked at a watch that instantaneously appeared on his wrist. "We need to get back to purgatory. Busy, busy. Lots of things to do."

"You guys don't do anything but stand around and wait," Eshu told him. "There's nothing to do in purgatory. Nothing."

I elbowed him again, eager to get out of here before he started a fight—especially since we'd just narrowly avoided a war.

Remiel stood. "This matter is not over, it's only postponed. If Maude Hoffman does not appear in heaven after her death, then we will file a grievance."

After threatening war, filing a grievance sounded good to me. I lifted my coffee cup to the angels, and nodded as they all vanished, leaving Eshu and me sitting at the table alone.

"I'm guessing that Maude Hoffman will not go to heaven after her death?" Eshu asked, passing me his flask.

I poured some of the contents in my coffee then passed it back. "Maude Hoffman died in 1984. Ann Fleming may go to heaven, although she is currently interested in learning more about her other options, such as Hades's Underworld."

Eshu chuckled. "Poacher."

I shrugged. "It's a free world, before death and after death."

"True." Eshu drained his coffee cup and stood. "I've got five messages to deliver to the wrong people. Wanna come with me?"

I sipped my coffee. "No thanks. We're breaking ground on the new Cliffs of Despair, then this afternoon Babylon and I are taking Ann to the MVA for her driver's license. She's got a job—two jobs actually. She's working at the bar with Babylon, then has some sales job on the side."

"Have fun. You'll probably need this. The MVA is hell." Eshu set the flask down on the table beside my coffee. "See you at dinner Sunday?"

I smiled, thinking how amazing life had become. Simple things like Sunday dinner with a loud, boisterous family weren't something I ever thought I'd enjoy, but I found those weekly dinners amazing. Because Babylon was there. Any moment I spent with her was a moment I cherished.

"See you at dinner," I told Eshu.

He vanished. I drank my coffee. And I pocketed the flask as I paid up and left the Bob Evans, because Eshu was right. The MVA was hell.

And sadly, it wasn't a hell I'd designed.

# EPILOGUE

"Coming, coming!" Rita called as she ran down the stairs to the front door. Who on earth would come all the way down the lane to her family farmhouse in the middle of the day like this.

She flung open the door and couldn't help but smile back at the attractive woman with reddish blonde hair and freckles. Another woman stepped into view, and Rita's smile widened.

"Babylon! What a surprise! Come in. I'll put on a pot of coffee. Oh, and I made some of my great grandmother's peach crumble last night. It's a famous family recipe, you know."

"We'd love some." Babylon put her hand on the other woman's shoulder. "I wanted to introduce you to a distant cousin of mine, as well as to ask a favor. Rita Hoffman, this is Ann Flemming. She just moved here from out of state and I was hoping she could practice her sales pitch and make-over skills on you."

Rita looked at the pink box that Ann held, gripped tight

in a nervous hand. "Oh, Mary Kay! I love their products and would be happy to be your make-over and sales-pitch victim...er practice dummy? I might even buy some moisturizer."

"Thank you." Ann smiled nervously, shifting the case to her other hand. "I need the practice. I haven't done this sort of thing in...well, in a very long time."

Rita opened the door wide. "Then, come on in. We'll talk over coffee and peach crumble." She looked at the other woman, frowning for a second before laughing. "You're going to think I'm crazy, but it's almost like I recognize you. You seem so familiar, and it took me a second to realize that you look just like my great grandmother, Mary Ann Hoffman. She went by Maude. I never knew her—she died before I was born. But you look just like pictures of her."

"Oh I get that all the time." Ann blushed and lifted a hand to her cheek. "I mean, people thinking I look like someone else, not people telling me I look like your great grandmother."

Rita led them into the kitchen. "Isn't it funny how some people bear a striking resemblance, but they're not related at all? Although my great grandmother's maiden name was Flemming, so maybe you are distantly related after all. Still, it makes me wonder about reincarnation, you know. Well, have a seat both of you. Ann, you go ahead and get your supplies out and I'll put on the coffee."

Funny how she felt as if she knew this woman. It wasn't just that Ann reminded her of her great grandmother, either. Maybe it was because she was a relative of Babylon's and they were close friends? Or maybe it was something else. Either way, Rita got the feeling Ann was going to be a good friend, someone she remained close to and loved for the rest of her life.

"Oh, and I'll get that peach crumble for us," Rita said as she grabbed the coffee pot. "You're going to love it."

Ann smiled. "I'm sure I will. In fact, I'm absolutely positive I'll think it's the best peach crumble I've ever had."

\* \* \*

FIND OUT ABOUT SALES, giveaways, and new releases, and ALL the shenanigans by signing up for my newsletter!

ALSO BY DEBRA DUNBAR

\* \* \*

<u>California Demon Series</u>

California Demon

Sinners on Sunset

Ventura Hellway

The Devil Went Down to Glendale

\* \* \*

<u>Half-breed Series</u>

Demons of Desire

Sins of the Flesh

Cornucopia

Unholy Pleasures

City of Lust

\* \* \*

<u>Imp World Novels</u>

No Man's Land

Stolen Souls

Three Wishes

Northern Lights

Far From Center

Penance

\* \* \*

<u>Northern Wolves</u>

Juneau to Kenai

Rogue

Winter Fae

Bad Seed

\* \* \*

<u>The Templar Series</u>

Dead Rising

Last Breath

Bare Bones

Famine's Feast

Royal Blood

Dark Crossroads

\* \* \*

<u>White Lightning Series</u>

Wooden Nickels

Bum's Rush

Clip Joint

Jake Walk

Trouble Boys

Packing Heat (TBD)

## ABOUT THE AUTHOR

Debra lives in a little house in the woods of Maryland with her sons and two slobbery bloodhounds. On a good day, she jogs and horseback rides, hopefully managing to keep the horse between herself and the ground. Her only known super power is 'Identify Roadkill'.

For more information:
www.debradunbar.com

## ACKNOWLEDGMENTS

Huge thanks to my copyeditor Kimberly Cannon, whose eagle eyes catch the typos and keep my comma problem in line, and to Rene George for once again providing me with an amazing cover design.

Printed in the USA
CPSIA information can be obtained
at www.ICGtesting.com
CBHW021017090924
14285CB00006B/30

9 781952 216442